PROMISES

PROMISES

DENNIS ROWE

TATE PUBLISHING
AND ENTERPRISES, LLC

Published by Tate Publishing & Enterprises, LLC
127 E. Trade Center Terrace | Mustang, Oklahoma 73064 USA
1.888.361.9473 | www.tatepublishing.com

Tate Publishing is committed to excellence in the publishing industry. The company reflects the philosophy established by the founders, based on Psalm 68:11,
"The Lord gave the word and great was the company of those who published it."

Book design copyright © 2015 by Tate Publishing, LLC. All rights reserved.
Cover design by Samson Lim
Interior design by Mary Jean Archival

Published in the United States of America

ISBN: 978-1-68028-405-8
Fiction / Biographical
15.02.16

To the memories of my mother, father, and their families as they struggled with the trials and hardships of the Great Depression and World War II, relying on their faith in God to see them through.

Acknowledgments

Thanks to my wife, Gabby, for her patience and loving support and to Debbie Causevic for her advice and mentoring during the process of writing this book.

Contents

1   Monsters and Rag Dolls.............................11

2   The Boy in the Stairwell 18

3   A Forever of Days 27

4   Roustabout 36

5   A Very Good Day.......................................42

6   A Cold Storm...52

7   The House behind the School 59

8   A Wedge of Wood.....................................68

9   A New Beginning.......................................77

10 Man of the House 85

11 The Buffoon...95

12 A Reunion of Sorts...................................106

13 The Boy at the Store.................................117

14 Worse than a Burr 127

15 In the Stairwell Again 138

16 War, Graduation, and Marriage...............147

17 The Most Important Thing.......................155

18	Bivouac	168
19	Birth and Survival	183
20	A Real Family	189
21	The Fall	194
22	Coming Home	208
Epilogue		211

Monsters and Rag Dolls

It had been foolish to worry about the monsters hiding under her bed. Her daddy had been telling the truth when he tucked her in and peeked underneath at her request. He assured her that nothing took up residence there aside from the dust balls and splintery wood floor planks.

Monsters would never hide. They had no need of it. Emma sensed that now that her world was falling apart. You knew when they were present. They announced themselves loudly enough that it left you in no doubt of their existence.

Fear numbed her limbs almost immobile as her father's steady hands scooped her into his arms. He pulled her tightly to his chest as he folded his large form through the open bedroom window like a magic trick. With hands as rough as leather, he gripped tightly onto the frayed rope that disappeared into the floodwaters surrounding the house.

"Just hang on to me, sweetheart. That there is the only job you have. Just hold on to me tight and close your eyes."

Emma kept her arms and legs locked like a vise around her father as he instructed, but her eyes defied him and remained wide open. From the second-story window of their tenement house, the little johnboat waiting below looked no bigger or stronger than a matchbox. Her mother and baby sister, Billie Lee, were already hunkered down in it as it vacillated below, held in place by the efforts of two men Emma had never seen before.

Even in the darkness of the night, Emma's gaze took in the whiteness of her mother's knuckles clutching the side of the boat. Her mother's pale face was turned upward as she watched their descent, a tense smile frozen on her face. Even at six, Emma understood that the smile was meant for her and that it was meant to be comforting.

She and her father were suspended halfway between the first and second story—her dad having paused to catch his breath—when the creaking and groaning started up like a new monster springing to life. A grunt of frustration or fear escaped her father as he resumed their descent. He methodically placed one hand under the next, inching them closer to the sea of water below. Gradually, impossibly, they neared the little boat and the vast, rushing floodwaters.

"Almost there, sweetheart," her daddy attempted to assure her, his voice hoarse from strain.

There were other boats and other men in the darkness, laboring in the pitching floodwaters to save other families as well. The pale yellow lights of their lanterns announced their locations like the fireflies of midsummer.

The groaning grew stronger, drowning out the sloshing of the brown water that was filling up the world. A bobbing movement in the water caught Emma's eye. The long, irregular object that approached looked like it had grotesque arms and fluffy white gloves. The water carried the object straight into the side of the johnboat, whacking its side so that the boat rocked precariously, nearly dumping its passengers—two men, her mother, and her baby sister—into the flood's bowels. When the bizarre object skirted around the boat and passed underneath them, Emma realized that the fluffy white gloves were in fact small, wet bundles of cherry blossoms attached to a large branch or a small tree.

Her mother's ensuing scream was drowned out by the groaning. To Emma's horror, she suddenly understood that the sound was coming from their home, as if it was protesting their hurried departure.

"Don't look, Emma Jo," her father repeated as one of the men below started grabbing for his legs.

When Emma felt their bodies lurch as if they were on a tire swing, she listened and closed her eyes tight. For a terrifying second, they were airborne, and then she felt a painful thump, followed by a comforting rocking, and heard her mother's half-suppressed sobs of relief.

Keeping her eyes pressed shut, Emma felt herself being deposited into her mother's arms and squished against her baby sister who was attempting to outbellow the storm. Below her, the boat started moving, carrying her family to safety. Emma didn't move or make a sound as she tried not to think of monsters. Around her, her mother sobbed, Billie Lee howled, and her father worked to catch his breath.

Then, from up above them and all around, came a terrible creaking *whoosh*. Emma's eyes opened despite her desire to keep them shut. In the hazy yellow lights of the lanterns, the sight of her family's tenement house collapsing down into the water like a cardboard box greeted her as it gave way to the monster that had come from the river. The house closed in upon itself with such ease that Emma found herself marveling over how it had ever been strong enough to hold them at all.

The monster from the river was bigger than anything Emma had ever imagined while trying to fall asleep that night. The monster from the river was born from the monster in the sky. From the relentless rains of winter that continued into spring, it touched everything with its cold, lifeless fingers. Emma believed that where one monster lingered, more would arise. So was the case with the monster from the river.

She had heard the grownups talking about its coming for weeks now. Their hope was that the levees would hold it back, keep it channeled here and moving south. There was hushed-up talk of packing and leaving for higher ground. But no one left because everyone thought the levees could contain it.

Emma's breath hitched as she thought of the rag dolls that her father had made her set back down on her bed after he had laboriously hoisted himself back up the rope from helping her mama and baby sister onto the boat. The look he had given her had been kind and sorrowful, but firm, as he bent down and extracted her dolls' soiled and worn bodies from her clenched fingers. With a whisper, he admitted that he feared she might fall into the water if she held on to anything aside from him.

Tears stung her eyes as she watched the house her mother had sometimes called their "shabby little nothing" sink down into the water and float away in the current of the beast. It was the thought of her dolls sinking down into the blackness of a cold and watery death that made Emma's tears finally start to flow.

She pulled away from her mama and from the howls of baby Billie and wrapped her small body up into the tightest ball she could manage. She clasped her hands over her ears and smashed her eyes closed once again. Even so, the smell of the beast that was the floodwater surrounding them and sloshing about in the bottom of the johnboat filled her nose. It was a dirty smell, full of the death of houses and trees and favorite rag dolls. Emma would never forget it as long as she lived.

—◅◅◅◦◦◦◦▻▻▻—

The gymnasium of East Prairie's new two-story school, R. A. Doyle Elementary, was dank and unpleasant. The room was filled with the smell of sweat and fear that spilled off the newly homeless bodies that crowded into it. Emma scanned the room that was full of unfamiliar faces; each one was taut with fear and tension. In seeing them, she realized that more people in East Prairie had lost their homes than she had known to have lived in the endless farmlands surrounding the town.

Like her father, many of the men were sharecroppers, toughened by labor and colored by the sun. They were used to the backbreaking hours that stretched clear from dawn until dusk most days of their lives. In an attempt to avoid the sorrow filling the room, Emma huddled close behind her father and moved about the room along with him. Before long, he noticed her shadow and instructed that she return to her mother over on the cots. He had overheard that kindhearted strangers were passing out dry clothes to the flood victims. He was attempting to secure some.

Obediently, Emma returned to her mother and sank down onto the cot next to her. She was rocking little Billie Lee, who had fallen into a fitful sleep. Freeing one hand, her mother reached out and allowed her fingers to sink deep into Emma's damp tangle of thick, coal-black hair.

"You're plum soaked to the core, Emma Jo," she stated. Her voice sounded hollow and tinny, unnatural compared to her usual singsong tones.

"There's no getting our stuff back now, Mama, is there?"

She was silent for so long that Emma thought she hadn't heard her over the din of commotion in the room. "No, baby girl, there ain't no getting it back."

"Do you think my dolls sank down into the mud, or do you think they'll keep going on to New Orleans and dump out into the ocean?"

"I wish I knew. All we had was gone so fast, it's like it never existed at all. I keep thinking about all them pictures we had. I thought pictures froze us in time forever, but it turns out they didn't after all."

Before long, Emma spotted her father making his way through the crowd. Like the other men filling the room, he was lean and strong from his years of sharecropping. Her father, however, was tall, and he moved with a certain grace that set him apart from the others. Under his arm was a folded mass of material. Emma shivered at the idea of changing into someone else's clothes, even if they were dry. She liked wearing her own dresses. She was used to the way they rubbed up against her skin and hugged her not too tightly under her armpits.

Obliged to obey her father, Emma stripped out of her wet dress and into a warm faded blue one that was worn thin at the sides. Thankfully, it hugged her skin in comfort. Her mother passed Billie to her father's arms and left to change behind one of the privacy partitions that were being erected.

"You okay, Emma Jo?" her father asked, his hazel eyes passing over her in concern.

It was in response to his question that Emma felt her chin quivering like it had a mind of its own and didn't know she had promised herself she was done crying. *Right as rain*, she wanted to say, but she managed to hold back the words. She would never say those words again if she could help herself. Rain was only right until it was wrong, and then it quickly became the worst wrong in the world.

"I'm awfully sorry I had to stop you from taking your dolls, sweetheart. I needed to get you down that rope, and I didn't know how else to do it."

"It's okay, Daddy. They were nothing but rag dolls anyway."

"You know, when this is over, there's going to be a whole heap of rags. Your mama will help you make new ones when the time is right."

Emma nodded and pinched her chin between her thumb and forefinger to try to keep it from quivering.

"There's a blanket here. Why don't you try to catch some shut-eye, baby? The night's going to be long enough as it is."

With nothing else to do, Emma slipped underneath the foreign-smelling blanket and took in several slow, even breaths. Was it just a few nights ago that Emma had last asked her father to check under the bed for her? How silly she had been, she thought, as she allowed her body to sink into the foggy darkness that beckoned her. When monsters were about, they were never hiding. She understood that now, and she would never forget it either.

The Boy in the Stairwell

The floodwater that snaked itself around all but the highest points in town proved to be in no hurry to leave. After being confined to the school for a few days, Emma felt that a new way of living was presenting itself. The grown-ups milled about—the women lamenting over the possessions they had lost, the men talking about the flood and, before long, cotton.

Like the stinky cigarettes her father craved, cotton had become as important to the men of East Prairie as air. At various times, the farmers and sharecroppers calling this town home scorned it with a passion close to the devil himself. It was their living, however, and they couldn't take their minds off it for long. While the women mourned their lost photographs and heirlooms, the men tired of talking about the swell of the water that the levees had not been able to contain now lurking over the fields—laying a bizarre claim on them—and turned back to talking about cotton.

It was late April, and so long as the fields were dry within a month or so, they could still be planted this year. There, in the gentle stirrings of words that passed from mouth to mouth, hope was born again. For everyone knew what the floodwaters brought with them. New soil. And new soil could be a very good thing.

Tired of the grown-ups' talk, Emma passed the days playing with the children of the other sharecroppers and flood victims and entertaining baby Billie when her mother demanded it. She loved making her baby sister laugh. It was an infectious sound that made a peculiar glow bubble up in her own chest. Emma eventually grew tired of Billie's continued persistence at repetition. No matter how many times Emma pulled her mouth into an O and crossed her eyes, Billie would laugh and point her finger at Emma like she was the cat's meow.

"Mama, can I go play?" Emma asked, pulling her attention away from Billie even though doing so made her little sister's lips stick out in a pout. To soften the blow, she first reached out and gave her sister's plump little thigh a playful squeeze, causing another hearty giggle to spill forth into the bustling afternoon.

"Why don't you?" her mother agreed. "I'll see if I can get Billie Lee to nap a bit. I'm betting she's cutting teeth as cranky as she is today when you aren't doting on her."

Emma jumped off the cot and circled the room in search of the two girls she most liked to play with. They were cousins to one another and older than Emma by a few years. Emma found she envied them. They were terribly pretty girls and knew just how to sass one another enough to make Emma almost pee her pants in laughter.

Halfway through the circle, she spotted her father talking to a small group of men. His back was to her, and his hands were clasped behind him. Feeling brave, Emma snuck over and tugged on one of his fingers. He turned, saw her, and winked.

"Ya'll right, Emma Jo?"

"Yes, Papa. I'm just looking to play."

"Well, have at it," he said, ruffling her hair.

Emma circled the room twice more, but she couldn't find the two cousins anywhere. Pushing open a door on the far side of the room, she peaked into a stairwell, found it empty aside from its echo, and stepped inside. The steps of the stairwell were concrete, wide, and inviting. She busied herself playing her own version of upstairs-downstairs hopscotch, bounding up and down the stairs while alternating legs and hops. It felt good to move, and pretty soon, she could feel a few locks of her black hair sticking to the back of her neck.

She gasped in surprise when she looked up once and saw a boy about her age watching her from the bend in the staircase up above. Halfway up the first set of stairs, she turned and started fleeing for the bottom.

Her fingers were closing over the door to the gymnasium when he called down to her. "I didn't mean to scare you none."

Emma paused and looked up the staircase, but she couldn't see him from where she stood. "Then why didn't you say you were there?" she retorted.

"Because you were busy hopping," he replied, peeking his head over the rail to look at her.

"What are you doing in here?"

"Well, I wasn't hopping, that's for sure."

Boys, Emma thought, shaking her head in disgust and turning back toward to the door. They didn't know how to give you a straight answer for anything.

"Want to see something?" the boy called as she pulled on the door to leave.

"See what?" she asked, pausing and looking up at him. He had olive skin, dark, wavy hair, and brown eyes. She figured he was right about her age.

"Come on up here and you can see for yourself."

"It'd better be good," Emma said, letting go of the door and beginning the ascent toward him.

"Why? Don't you like stairs unless you are hopping up them?"

"I like stairs just fine. I just don't like to waste my time."

He huffed as she approached. "What have you got to do here *but* waste time?"

"Well, what is it?" she asked, pausing a few steps below him and setting her hands on her hips. Truth be told, Emma didn't know any boys particularly well aside from her father, and being around them always made her skin feel prickly.

"Out here," he replied, turning and jogging up the second flight of stairs. When he reached the top, he pushed open a big, metal door.

"Are you sure you should go out there?" Emma asked, as sunlight poured into the stairwell. It had stopped raining at least. She had been beginning to fear it would never stop raining and they'd all drown without an ark to save them.

"What else is there to do?"

Emma frowned. The truth was there wasn't anything else to do. With one last glance down the empty stairwell, she followed him out onto the roof. The heavy door shut behind her with a peculiar finality.

"See," he said, looking across the long, flat roof into the distance.

Emma followed his gaze and frowned deeper. She had heard of mountains so vast and high you couldn't see their peaks from standing at their base. East Prairie, however, was likely the flattest place on earth. Looking out over the roof, it felt like you could see forever.

And forever, unfortunately, was filled with water.

Emma felt her stomach flip when she wondered where exactly out there the remains of her home and bed were floating. Would her bedsheets turn up in a hickory tree, or would they be swallowed by a shark down in the Gulf of Mexico?

"You brought me up here to see water," Emma said, trying to sound more unimpressed than afraid. She wondered if she would hate water forever. All around her, the water looked like a monster that had struck land and was now dying a slow death.

Beside her, the boy shrugged. "Go back down if you don't like it."

"I will," she said, tossing her hair a bit too dramatically as she headed for the heavy metal door.

Her stomach lurched into a tighter ball when the knob refused to turn at her request. "It's locked," she said, trying to keep the fear closed up in her belly and out of her voice.

"Quit your funny business," the boy said, walking up beside her and trying it himself. "Damn."

"You shouldn't cuss," Emma said reflexively. "You'll go to the devil if you do."

"You'll be cussing when we are stuck out here for hours and no one comes up to rescue us."

"What makes you think it will be hours before someone finds us?"

"Because I was sitting there for hours and no one came into the stairwell 'cept you, that's why."

Setting her hands on her hips in frustration, Emma studied the roof, looking for another way down. She found there wasn't one.

"What are you doing?" the boy asked, hovering near the door.

"Looking for another door," Emma replied nonchalantly.

There was a second door on the far end of the roof, but Emma's investigations found it just as locked as the first. Kicking at the loose gravel with her bare toe, she tried not to let her gaze travel out over the roof toward the endless water in the distance.

"Well, that's just horse feathers. How come you didn't get stuck out here when you first found this place?" she accused him on her return approach. For some reason, he was still hovering near the locked door.

"I just didn't."

"Are you playing a trick on me?" she asked, poking his chest with one finger and narrowing her eyes. "'Cause if you are, I'll tell my daddy, and he's got a temper like you've never seen when it comes to mean boys."

"I'm not playing a trick on you, and I'm not mean either. I didn't get stuck then, well, because I don't like heights. I didn't come out so far when I was alone."

"Boys," Emma said, turning away from him to survey the roof again.

"What do you mean 'boys'?"

"I just don't like boys, that's all."

"That's the dumbest thing I ever heard. How can you not like boys? The world's half-full of boys."

"Not my half."

That was when Emma spotted the red metal rungs sticking up from the brick on the far side of the roof. She crossed over determinedly, the boy following not far behind. As she suspected, it was a fire escape that led to the ground two stories below. Her belly did a complete flip at the idea of crossing over the thick brick wall and having to clamber down it, but it would be better than being stuck up here with a boy until they were rescued.

Besides, she felt sure her daddy would have at her backside good for following some boy up onto the roof. He didn't spank her often, but when he did, it served to remind her that she could do without his spankings the rest of her life. If she could get down quick, he'd never have to know.

"You aren't going to try it, are you?" the boy asked, wiping a bead of sweat from his brow. "Those fire escapes never reach the ground, you know. You'll have to jump the final six feet or so."

"I ain't keen on being stuck up here, are you?"

"I'm a little less keen on heights."

"I've seen you down below, haven't I? Your mom is the littlest woman I ever saw, and you've got a passel of brothers and sisters, haven't you?"

He scowled and dropped her gaze.

"Well, are we going or aren't we?" Emma asked, drying her palms on her borrowed dress.

"I reckon we're going," he replied. "If I fall, don't follow me."

"Fiddlesticks," Emma said, slipping between the boy and the thin rungs of the ladder to go down before him. "A boy who is afraid of heights ain't no better at this than a girl."

The worst part, Emma found, was crossing over the thickness of the brick wall and slipping her body around until it was vertical on the thin metal rungs of the fire escape. Gallantly, the boy tried to lean over to hold her by the elbow until she was stable. Emma paused long enough to pull her elbow free. "You're making me more scared doing that, not less."

When she wasn't more than five or six steps down, she heard him scuttling about above her, and then he appeared on the ladder straight above. For the first time, she noticed that his feet were as bare as hers.

"Don't you dare fall on me," she snapped and hurried her own descent. As the boy had predicted, the final rung ended several feet above the ground. Like a monkey, Emma scooted her body downwards on the rungs until she was hanging by her hands on the final rung. Hanging from there, it didn't feel like such a far drop.

Finally, her hands screaming from hanging suspended for so long, Emma let herself fall. She landed in the grass in a heap, and while everything smarted, she knew she wasn't hurt.

She scooted out of the way and waited for the boy to drop as well. He couldn't quite figure out how to maneuver on the ladder the same way, and he ended up dropping from several feet higher. He winced and rubbed his ankle.

"You okay?" she asked.

"'Course I'm okay," he said, standing up and brushing his palms on the back of his worn pants. "There's a side door down here that's never locked," he said, waving her along.

Emma stood up and followed him around the school. He pulled open one of the doors on the side of the building and motioned her inside.

"I guess that wasn't too bad," Emma said, stepping between the boy and the frame of the door that he was holding open for her.

"What's your name?" he asked.

"Emma. What's yours?"

"Ray."

She nodded and shoved a thick lock of hair behind one ear. "Well, I'm sorry, I just don't like boys." Then she turned and ran inside to find her father.

A Forever of Days

Later that afternoon, Ray sat on the cot and surveyed his family. Emma's words rang in his ears. His mother was little; it was true. And, for being the oldest at six years of age, he did have a lot of little brothers and sisters.

Ever since he could remember, his family had lived in labor camps along the Mississippi River. Ray's father was strong and more than capable of the incessant work that came with taming the mighty river.

Many of the laborers living in camps were young men with no families at all. But enough of them were like his father, providing for families of their own by giving them a simple, small community life along the banks of the river. Ray knew plenty of those families. Other mothers, fathers, and children. He was sad to admit it, but that ornery girl with the coal-black hair and bright blue eyes had been right.

His mother was the shortest mother of them all. In contrast to his father, who was tall and strong, his mother seemed little bigger than a child herself. More often than not, her belly was round and filled with yet another sibling, just as she was when the river swelled over its banks, causing their entire community to flee for safety.

Some of the laborers, like the sharecroppers, hadn't been able to flee fast enough. Ray had heard that many of them likely drowned. Others were ushered by the authorities onto barges to wait out the flood.

Ray was thankful his family got out, and he wasn't one to complain as to the way his life tended to present itself. He didn't mind living indoors as he was now doing. It was different than the tent-living in camp that he was used to. Sleeping indoors closed you off from the earth and the sky. The rain didn't seep in as it did through the holes in the canvas or push up through the splintery plank floor as it sometimes did. Nor did the chill in the night air soak through your blankets. The solid walls of the school didn't budge in the wind no matter how hard it blew.

The heat of the day when it was sunny outside, however, eventually found its way in through the open windows of the school. It didn't relinquish either until all the bodies packed inside the gymnasium had been silent and still in the night for a very long time.

What Ray didn't like was the feeling of confinement that rose up inside him from being packed in with so many people. When Ray looked into his father's dark, restless eyes, he knew that he felt the very same way. There was a visible edginess setting up in his father as the days wore on inside the school. His father's hands badly needed to be at work again.

It was on the banks of the river that his father felt most at home. Here in the school, he was lost and useless. Making idle conversation was not his strong suit. He preferred heading out to the river shortly after first light and spending the length of his day in an unending attempt to tame something that would likely never be tamed, no matter what people hoped. Leastwise, that was what his father often said. Dams and bridges could be built, and slews could be dredged. But when the mighty Mississippi wanted it, she would rise up and have her say, just as she was doing now.

Everyone who knew Ray's father knew that he carried with him an uncommon strength. One day, Ray had ventured to ask his father how he came to be so strong. He had ruffled his hair and told him that he pulled his strength straight from the river, the same way trees pull water from the ground. He said as long as his life was by the river, he would never run out of strength.

Seeing the way his mother relaxed inside the school, Ray couldn't help but wonder if his mother loved the river in the same way his father did. He had never asked her, but if he did, and if she was truthful, Ray suspected she would have said no even before the flood. Ray had a hunch his mother drew her strength from his father, the way she clearly set store on him. Maybe it was because she was so small that she didn't need to set store in something as big and fierce as a river. Maybe because she was so small, it was easier for her to pull her strength from a person.

Sometimes Ray found himself wondering what he would pull his strength from when he got bigger. He couldn't venture to even guess at that. However, when he stood on the river's banks and took in the endless meandering water that slid down from the north and traveled south as far as the eye could see—when he pulled in the scent of muddy water that was as familiar to him as the smell of bacon frying in a pan—Ray doubted he would be able find his strength in it.

Considering the way he felt more lost and alone the more crowded the gymnasium became, he doubted he would find his strength in people either. That was why he had come to be on the steps earlier that morning when Emma had come in, fixed on her hopping game and not taking notice of him just a dozen or so feet above her.

She didn't like boys, she had said. Well, maybe he didn't like girls either. Not ornery ones like her, anyway. There were plenty of girls in camp, just like there were plenty of boys.

As a general rule, boys were more fun. They could run faster and climb trees higher, and they almost never fell to the ground pretending to have hurt their ankles when you were about to close in on them in a game of chase either.

He shouldn't have let her get under his skin. His father was always saying never to let anything get under your skin but the rays of the sun. He didn't know why it bothered him so much—the smarty-pants way she had referred to his mother and his brothers and sisters. She was just a silly girl after all. Ray knew there were people he needed to pay mind to and people he didn't. Emma, no matter how much braver she was than him, was one of those people whose opinions didn't need to account for anything in his world.

◦⫘⫘◦

By the time a forever of days passed into weeks, and weeks tumbled into one another, the earth had finally soaked in enough of the water along the banks of the Mississippi that it was time for the Rowe family to get home. *Home* was a relative term as far as Ray's father was concerned. The only true condition that defined the word was that it was alongside the river. The particular town they were living in never mattered. Ray's father went wherever work on the river could be gotten, and he worked for whichever company was hiring when work ran dry.

Three days after the girl with her coal-black hair—who had somehow gotten under his skin just like the rays of the sun—left the school with her family, Ray helped his mama herd his brothers and sisters onto the train that would take them to Arkansas.

There was going to be an endless amount of work to do on the river now, his father said with just the smallest of gleams in his eye. With all the clearing and dredging and repairing of levees and embankments, there was likely to be work for years to come. The adults kept talking about how they were living through the biggest flood in history. In some places, they said, the Mighty Mississippi was still seventy miles wide. There was a lot of sour talk aimed against President Coolidge, who, despite the requests of countless mayors, governors, and other officials, refused to visit the waterlogged midlands of America. In Coolidge's absence, Secretary of Commerce Herbert Hoover became a favorite of the farmers, sharecroppers, and other displaced Americans for his efforts to bring aid to the Midwest.

From the window of the train, Ray spotted the R. A. Doyle Elementary School that had been his home for such an unexpected stretch of time. He didn't figure he'd ever see it or the town again, not with them heading down to Arkansas as they were. As long as his father had any say, Ray's life was going to be next to the Mississippi, drinking in her smell at night and the smell of his mama frying up bacon in the morning.

With his little sister howling in his ear, Ray watched the school until the train rolled them out of its sight. He pressed his fingers to the glass and mumbled good-bye, an unexpected nostalgia rushing over him.

He thought of the girl with the bouncy black hair rushing over to him abruptly to say good-bye before departing with her own family. They hadn't spoken or acknowledged one another in weeks, and Ray found her approach to be anything but expected. She had been spending her time with two older girls who Ray thought were as silly as girls could get. He himself had gotten around to making friends with a few of the boys his age as well.

She had half-run, half-skipped her way over to him. When she came to an abrupt stop right in front of him, her bouncy curls had drawn his gaze in a peculiar way.

"We never got caught," she had said, holding the lower part of her dress out with her thumbs in a way that reminded him of a curtsey.

Ray wrinkled his brow. For some reason, he was at a loss for words.

"I thought for sure we would have," she continued.

"But you don't like boys," Ray replied, finally having found his voice and immediately wishing he hadn't.

"No, but I still thought maybe I should say good-bye, considering…"

"Considering what?" Ray asked when she paused.

She shrugged her thin shoulders. "Considering it was kind of fun, I reckon."

"I reckon it was 'cept for the part about the heights."

She giggled—an infectious, bubbly laugh that lit up her blue eyes.

"You leaving?" Ray asked, noticing that they had the attention of the girl's parents as they hovered near the door.

"Yeah, my daddy got work at a cotton gin."

"Well then, good-bye, Emma."

She laughed a second time, and Ray had the distinct feeling she was laughing at him. "Maybe I'll see you again."

"It ain't likely. My pa works on the river. We're headed to Arkansas in a few more days."

"I wouldn't work on a river if it was the last job on earth."

Ray scowled and started to turn away when she stopped him by closing her small hand over his arm.

"I just meant that I hate water the way you hate heights, that's all."

She ran back to her parents then, and Ray had watched her go with a very strange feeling in the pit of his stomach.

———

Arkansas turned out to be no different than southern Missouri, with the exception that the summer felt even hotter and more humid, which almost seemed impossible. At least Ray's father promised that winters in the tent wouldn't be as long or as dreary this much farther south as they were.

As his father had predicted, there would be work taming back the river for years to come. Some of her harsh bends were going to be straightened and smoothed, promising the water an easier route to the Gulf. Levees were going to be enforced and enlarged. Marshes and forests needed to be cleared. It was tiresome work for certain, but since his father drew his strength from the river, Ray figured he was able to handle it better than most.

There were schools set up in most of the Mississippi River communities, and this proved true on the wide, fertile banks of northern Arkansas. Usually these schools were taught by camp wives and held outside in good weather or in tents in bad weather. Now that Ray was six, he was old enough to attend. With him went Katherine, who was a year younger and the closest of his siblings in age.

Those first few months, he wasn't certain if he liked learning to read and write. It didn't come easily the way addition and subtraction did for him. Finally though, the letters and words began to click, and by the time he was eight, reading was as natural to him as breathing. The idea that at one point in his life he hadn't been able to do so seemed foreign and surreal.

Math continued to be his favorite subject as the years passed. Numbers just fell into place in his mind, and he often knew the answer as soon as his teacher finished reciting the question. Sometimes, when the nights were long and cold, he'd lay on his cot in the tent crowded next to one of his brothers and wonder if one day he'd draw his strength from numbers the way his father drew it from the river.

With each few years that passed, their tent grew more crowded. Ray loved his brothers and sisters, each and every one of them, despite how much space they took up in their crowded tent. There were nine in all, including himself. As a result, his mother needed all the help she could get. She loved them all, but he saw her sigh on occasion, perhaps daunted by all the mouths to feed and all the laundry to do. As a general rule, the Rowes didn't have much aside from their children to consider their own. All his father's endless hours of labor went to meet endless requirements of feeding and clothing their big family.

Enough money was usually scrounged up to buy everyone shoes or boots in winter. In the warmer months, most of his family went barefoot. Ray understood that his family was dirt-poor. He would have been a liar not to admit that on occasion it bothered him, just like all the caregiving he had to do to aid his overburdened mother.

As he grew, Ray became very certain of two things. Whatever he did in life, he was not willing to rely on the same backbreaking physical labor his father did to make ends meet. And he would never have more children than he could provide for. With his penchant for math, Ray even allowed himself to dream that he would find a way to do something that could utilize this skill.

4

Roustabout

Sometimes, even though Emma knew she shouldn't, she would pretend not to listen when her parents talked about "big-people" things. Often their conversation would prove boring, and soon she would stop listening. Other times, this proved to be a good way to know what was in store for her.

She learned, for instance, two days prior to his telling her, that her father had secured a job at a time when doing so was as challenging as finding a needle in a haystack. Not just any job either. Aaron Delphi, or Dick as everyone knew him, had been offered a job as a roustabout by none other than John McCracken.

Emma knew neither what a roustabout was nor why her father would drop his voice in enunciation when he spoke the name John McCracken. But she got the feeling that both of these were marks of importance for her father.

What she did know was that, for the time being, there were no crops for the sharecroppers to harvest when the sluggish floodwaters finally receded. Eventually, there would be seeds to sow when the fields dried up enough to plant them, but sowing seeds and harvesting cotton didn't require the same number of hands. And since the waters took so long to dissipate, the planting year was going to be a minimal one.

This made her father's procuring his position of a roustabout even more fortunate. At least that was what Emma gathered from the broken bits of conversation she picked up while playing with Billie Lee. Her father's good fortune came as no surprise to her. The fact that John McCracken had the good sense to recognize her father's abilities just proved he was as worthy a man as her father believed him to be.

John McCracken couldn't have anything on her father. Dick Givens was tall and strong and, according to her mother, as whip-smart as God would let any one man be. He had the kindest eyes of anyone in the world, and when he rested a hand on her shoulder, Emma felt that he could soothe all the problems in the world.

When he pulled Emma onto his knee to tell her news of his employment officially, she felt her chest swell with happiness at the pride she saw in his eyes. When he finished relaying the news, he ruffled her hair. "You may not know it, Emma Jo, but this is the best news we've had in years."

"How so, Papa? Is it 'cause being a roustabout is better than being a sharecropper?"

"How'd you know I was hired as a roustabout, Emma? Did your mama tell you already?"

Emma shrugged her thin shoulders. "I hear it when you say things, is all."

"If that's so, then I'll take care to talk quieter when I have private conversations with your mama." His tone was stern, but there was a twinkle of amusement in his eye.

"It doesn't matter what I'm doing when I hear your voice, Daddy. I have an urge to listen. Mama does too, I think."

"Both you girls set store to me more than I'm worth. That I know. I suspect that for your mama's part, it was 'cause she was hardly more than a girl herself when we were wed."

"How old was she?"

"Fifteen."

"Fifteen is old."

"Not old enough, Emma. If any suitors come calling for you even a day before you turn eighteen, I'll chase 'em off with a rifle. That I swear."

"Mama says never to swear."

"The point is, Emma, we'll be getting a place of our own again."

"Will it really be ours?"

Her father's face dropped so slightly that Emma barely took notice of it. "No, it'll belong to the McCracken Cotton Gin Company. A tenement house and most likely a shabby one at that. But your mama's been pining for a house of our own for some years now, and I intend to give her one as soon as I can, more natural disasters coming our way or not."

"How?"

"You mark my words, Emma. When we were stuck in that schoolhouse for so long, I had the opportunity to have a few conversations with a pretty important man. A few things I mentioned in passing impressed him enough to offer me employment in his gin. Considering he has his pick of dozens of able-bodied men, this ain't one impression I've made that I intend to take lightly. Heck, he practically helped settle East Prairie. You're too young to know it, but John McCracken has held about every important job in this town there is. He was a fire chief, a mayor, an editor, and even the president of a bank."

"Is he a roustabout, too?"

Dick laughed heartily. "No, baby, he isn't. Mr. McCracken owns the cotton gin. A roustabout just means I get to see to the equipment in the gin and that, if I want to stay, I'm going to need to prove my worth. Those years working on cars up in St. Louis helped me to understand engines the way your mama understands how to make the perfect loaf of bread out of just a few ingredients."

"I miss Mama's cooking." Emma could almost taste a slice of the warm bread that had been a staple at most meals back when her mother had had a kitchen to cook in.

Her father pressed his lips against Emma's temple. "Soon enough, Emma. Good things are coming our way. Your mama will be cooking up a storm again 'fore you know it."

⸺◦⸺

When the time came to tour what was to be their new home, Emma worked hard not to let her face fall as she took it in. Observing the way her mother's smile wavered slightly, Emma reached out for her free hand. The other one was busy holding Billie Lee up on her hip.

For so long now, they had lived in the shelter of the school. Emma had grown accustomed to hearing the noises of other people when she slept. Here, noticing the droppings that lined the window frames, Emma suspected she'd have to grow used to the noises of mice scurrying about the scuffed wood floors as she drifted off. Mice weren't so bad. Their faces were almost cute. But her mother feared them something terrible, and whenever there was a sighting of one, her mother was on edge for days. She claimed it was the way they scurried about behind the walls when you were awake and were so bold when you weren't.

What Emma didn't like were spiders. To her dismay, the rough-looking tenement house had more than its share of cobwebs. It was a small house with five rooms if you counted the water closet. Emma and Billie Lee would have their own room to sleep in. It was the smaller of the two bedrooms and had a broken door. But it had a window with a view of a tree, and in the tree was a bird's nest right in plain view of what would become Emma's bed. The other two rooms were the family room and kitchen.

There was a woodstove, a table, and a hutch in the kitchen. There was a sofa in the family room and beds in the others. The sofa had clearly been torn and restitched in several places, and the mattresses were sunken low in the middles. But these were all things they could claim as their own so long as her father held his job.

"It's a bit dilapidated," her father directed to her mother, a sheepish look on his face, "but we can clean it up right quick. Then there's a company store with everything we might need. We can furnish the kitchen with supplies and food with a payroll deduction or two. We'll be behind for a bit, but we'll turn it around in no time."

Emma wasn't too young to hear the plea in her father's words. For his sake, she summoned a cheeriness that she didn't entirely feel. "There's one thing we won't have to buy, Papa." She pointed to a pot on the floor in the corner. "Someone left us a giant cooking pot."

"Yes, Emma Jo, it looks like they did. Tell you what, leave it be for now. Once I shimmy up to the roof and fix the leak, we'll clean it up good and give it to your mama. She can use it to mix up the biggest loaf of bread ever."

Maggie, Emma's mother, smiled at her husband, and Emma noticed that her smile was once again reaching her eyes. "Dick, you've always been a sucker for a good loaf of bread, haven't you?"

"Well, your bread, for certain."

Emma felt a familiar sense of peace wash over her, seeing the way her parents worked to please one another. The love her parents had for one another made her feel safe the same way she did when her father's arms were wrapped around her. This house might not be the one her mother had been dreaming of, but it got them out of the shelter, and it kept them together and safe.

Emma remembered back to the night her father had rescued her from her room. Only minutes afterward, her house and everything they owned had been washed away. The thought of it made her feel cold and sick all over again. To ease her worries, she studied the repeating pattern of planks that covered the floor. She counted them out over and over. One, two, three, four, five, six—all staggered the same width apart. Then they began to repeat. It was a comfort to her to learn that the pattern repeated itself time and again until it reached the wall. As she studied the floor closer, she noticed occasional faces in the natural grain of the wood. The one by her toe seemed to be smiling at her.

It was enough, she decided, to have a floor that welcomed you and the promise of the biggest loaf of bread her mother could one day make. Once again, Emma had a place to call home.

5

A Very Good Day

There was a bald eagle soaring overhead as Ray and his father walked along the riverbank, rifles in hand, early that January morning. As the eagle teetered when the wind whipped about, the sunlight would catch it, lighting up its white head and fanned tail like they were white fire.

"What do you think it wants, following us like this?" Ray asked his pa.

Russell paused in his step to examine the bird. "Maybe it just wants us gone."

"Think you could shoot it, Pa?"

Russell studied it then nodded confidently. "I could," he continued, "but I won't."

"What do you think it would taste like?"

"Quail maybe. Just tougher."

"It sure is pretty, ain't it, Pa?"

"It sure is. I ain't never been one to take aim at something so noble as that."

"Mrs. Grace told us last year that Benjamin Franklin had wanted the turkey to be our national symbol, not the eagle."

His pa chuckled heartily. "Good thing it isn't. Wouldn't do for everybody and their mother to be hunting America's national symbol every chance they got, would it?"

"It would sure be nice if we could shoot a turkey today." Ray's hand went to his stomach absentmindedly. It was 1934, and America was knee-deep in a terrible depression. His father had been one of the fortunate ones and had managed to keep steady—though occasionally reduced—employment in one river town or another, which Ray's mother attributed to his strong work ethic. Many of Russell's friends and coworkers had long since been sent packing.

During this trying time in America, the Rowe family did their best to stretch Russell's meager earnings. Ray went hunting with his father every chance they got. Whatever they managed to hunt was the only meat they typically had. They lived in relatively wild and untamed parts of Arkansas. The nearest town at the moment was Chicot, and it was often miles away, depending on where Russell's work necessitated they set camp. Ray's mother, Mary, had taken to growing vegetables alongside the tent whenever they stayed in one campground long enough to do so.

Ray and his pa walked in silence for another half mile. Ray's toes were pressing into his boots—ones that were given to him after a friend had outgrown them—and nearly cutting off his circulation. Ray knew better than to complain about it. There wasn't money for new boots. When these grew too bothersome, he'd cut through the leather at the front. He'd make do with them through the rest of the winter.

Soon enough it would be spring, and he could forget about wearing boots altogether. *And you never know*, he thought, *things might very well be better next year.*

Placing his hand on Ray's shoulder, Russell guided Ray toward a thick band of trees away from the river. With a cry that was almost disappointed, the eagle stopped its pursuit and settled down onto a high branch of an old oak tree with a commanding view of the river.

"I've got a good feeling about today, son," Russell said, winking down at him.

"How so?"

"It ain't every day that an eagle will grace you with its presence for so long, is it?"

Ray shrugged and said that it wasn't. They walked nearly a mile longer in silence, and Ray tried not to focus on the rumbling in his stomach when his father gripped his shoulder.

In complete silence, he pointed to a break in the woods. There, pecking indiscriminately at the forest floor was a small flock of turkeys.

"Pick one of them on the left, and I'll pick on the right," his father whispered. "Nod when you're ready, and we'll shoot on three."

Taking a deep breath, Ray focused on what he felt was the easiest target. He steadied himself then nodded. After three seconds of practiced silence, their rifles went off simultaneously, sending the flock into frenzy.

With a whoop and a holler, Ray and his father charged into the melee. One, Russell's, had been silenced instantly. Ray's thrashed a few seconds then collapsed as well.

"I told you it was going to be a blessed day, didn't I?" Russell asked, slipping his rifle behind him and gathering up his prize.

"You were right, Pa. It's a very good day."

⎯⎯⫷⫸⎯⎯

By the time he was fourteen, Ray was beginning to grow accustomed to the fact that the girls in camp paid him more than his fair share of attention. Like his father, he had olive skin and dark hair. But unlike him, he was just of average height, a fact which he believed his mother's particularly short stature contributed to. Ray suspected it was possible that the girls liked him because of the care he gave to his siblings at different points of his day. Girls, his mother had reassured him time and time again, liked to see a young man who was courteous enough to look after his own siblings. He wondered if she just said this to encourage his assistance when he yearned to be free of the tent and preferred to run outdoors, where the sounds and smells of his little siblings weren't so oppressive.

They followed him everywhere, particularly the twins, Art and Don. They were ten years younger, and they set store to him something fearsome. At four, they were generally the most troublesome—with the exception of Cecil, who was the toddler and the youngest of the family. Ray secretly hoped Cecil would be the last baby his parents would have. His mother was getting on in her years for having children, and there was plum just no more room in the tent. Cecil wasn't a particularly bad baby, but he had been sick most of the long winter, and his cries had filled the tent the full duration of many long nights, causing the entire family to awaken groggy and ill-tempered.

Ray hadn't known it at the time, but the twins were following him the afternoon he had his first kiss. He hadn't known it was coming, or he'd have looked over his shoulder better to ascertain whether or not they were sneaking around like always. Her name was Sarah. She had only been in camp for a few months. Where her family had come from, Ray didn't rightly know. He suspected it was another camp, since her father was lean and hard like his, and her family was no better off than his own.

She had befriended the other girls right away, falling into the camp like she had been there forever. Even though she claimed that she hated camp life, she was one of three girls her age who was always finding something to giggle about. A good deal of the time, she was looking over her shoulder at him while she was doing so. She was several months older and had already turned fifteen, and that made Ray just a bit uncomfortable.

It was March and the sun had finally come out behind the clouds after several weeks of hiding. Ray had headed out for a walk, and Sarah had somehow found her way right next to him.

Being completely alone with her closed up his words, made his throat feel tight and uncomfortable, and turned his palms sweaty. As far as girls went, Ray figured she was as silly as they got. He walked with her along the riverbank, pulling at words like they were straws and hoping for a decently long string of them but only finding short, clipped ones that didn't suffice. She smiled and giggled into the uncomfortable silences and tossed her springy blond hair in hopes of enticing him.

As soon as the kiss was over, Ray couldn't remember if she had asked for it aloud, or if he had finally just kissed her because he knew full well it was what she wanted. Her lips were soft and supple against his, which made him wonder as to the human mouth's ability to be so versatile. With a mouth, you could eat, whistle, talk, and sing or even play certain instruments. Kissing, he figured, had to be the most peculiar thing you could do with it.

When he pulled away, she promptly leaned closer, hoping for another. Ray fumbled on, wondering how long it would have to last for her to feel satisfied. Almost to his relief, he heard the giggling snorts of the twins from behind a tree.

He pulled away and chucked a few rocks in their direction. When he turned back to Sarah, he found the words just as pathetically tied up in his throat as they had been before the kiss.

"I should go," he managed.

"I'll be seeing you, Ray," she replied, squeezing his hand and tossing her blond hair back over her shoulder.

Bounding with repressed energy, he chased the twins all the way back to the tent while they hollered like they were being chased by the devil himself.

They bounded through the closed canvas flaps of the tent, jarring the frame wickedly and waking Cecil from his nap. Ray pulled to a walk before entering, but the rapid rise and fall of his lungs and the sweat of his brow proved to his mother that he was the culprit responsible for the twins' unruly behavior.

They collapsed onto the wood floor of the tent in hysterics, making little smacking sounds with their lips. In his crib, Cecil began to cry.

Turning her mouth into a thin line, Mary pointed at the tent door and directed the boys back outside where they were told to stay until they could slip on their indoor manners.

"Honestly, Ray," Mary said, setting her hands on her hips after they had taken off at a run. "Why did you chase them in here? You know how Cecil needs his rest."

"I'm sorry, Ma, I wasn't thinking." Ray ran his fingers through his thick hair self-consciously, hoping his mother hadn't picked up on the boys' smacking sounds.

Mary glared up at him—he towered above her now—but the anger quickly fell out of her eyes. She turned and pulled Cecil from his crib—he had started sucking the back of his hand hungrily—and slipped him into his high chair.

"I need you to go into town for me, Ray. Cecil needs his medicine, and we're out of beans and nearly out of flour too."

Ray shrugged easily. He welcomed the long walk into town no matter how rutty and mucky the road was likely to be now that spring was on its way. It would abate the energy that was lingering in his veins after his kiss with Sarah. What a powerful and troubling thing kissing was, especially considering he didn't even much care for her.

"I reckon you want me to take that rickety old wagon then?"

"It won't be easy to haul everything back if you don't." Mary stepped outside, pulling open the double flaps of the tent and tying them to the posts. "What I really want is for you to take Cecil with you. This mangy old place could use some deep cleaning, and the Lord only knows how difficult it is for me to get it done with him clinging to me all day long."

"But it's practically five into town, and he's likely to cry the whole way," Ray protested.

"He likes the wagon just fine. Besides, the sun is finally shining, and it's promising to be a beautiful day. It'll be good for your brother. The winter's been hard on us all, for certain, but Cecil's had it awful rough with the crud in his lungs these long months. Just let me feed him first."

The sun was bright and high overhead when Ray finally took off, lugging the wagon and Cecil behind him. It was pleasant and warm for March, promising that spring was finally in the air. Every so often, a chill, light breeze pushed at Ray's bangs, promising him that winter would attempt to hang on a little while longer.

Wide awake, with a full belly, and pleased with the change of routine, Cecil sat up, leaned against the back of the wagon, and smiled and pointed at everything he saw. He cooed and chortled and made exclamations that Ray couldn't hope to understand. At just two, Cecil babbled an awful lot, but only their mother claimed to understand him. Ray suspected this had as much to do with the fact that Cecil was an adamant pointer as it was due to her unique mothering skills.

Cecil coughed as much as he laughed while the wagon jerked him along. Ray envisioned the jiggling of the wagon loosening the phlegm clinging to his chest and sending it on its way for good.

As they progressed down the long, rutted, and deserted dirt road into Chicot, Ray unleashed everything that was weighing on his mind to little Cecil. Cecil seemed to enjoy Ray's one-sided conversation. He even colored it with his own enthusiastic grunts. Ray vented for a mile about the silliness of girls in particular, insisting over and over that he was likely to never understand their intimate thoughts and desires. It would be easier if they were like mathematical equations: after devoting enough study and thought to them, he would be able to reach some finite understanding that explained how they thought and said and did the peculiar things they did.

"Take Mom and Dad for instance," Ray said, turning back to check on Cecil as one of the back wagon wheels dipped into a particularly deep rut. "You've never seen two people who understand one another better. Dad knows when Mom's in a surly mood as soon as he steps into the tent, even if she's facing the other way. And she knows when his back is hurting just from the way he takes a seat, regardless of the fact that he won't tell a soul when he's in pain. Somehow or another, they've figured each other out just like math equations."

Ray kicked at a dried-up pile of horse droppings with the toe of his newest pair of hand-me-down boots. This pair had cracks breaking through the soles and the leather was becoming unstitched at the base, but they fit and Ray figured wearing them was better than going barefoot until the winter was finished.

Ray's mother liked to say that she thanked the angels that, like his father, nothing got under Ray's skin or riled him unnecessarily. However, walking around the camp barefoot in a foot of snow or on a sheet of ice was one of the few things that could.

His thoughts returned to Sarah and her giggles and hair tossing. He doubted he could ever understand her the way his father understood his mother. He doubted he'd really want to either.

"What do you care, huh, Cecil?" Ray asked as they closed in on the final few miles into town. Ray was glad to be doing so because the clouds were coming in fast; they were blotting out the sun and increasing the bite that the wind carried. Cecil was starting to whine and shiver, and he was tired of being jiggled so much. "You don't have to worry about girls forever. By the time you do, the other eight of us will have it figured out, and we'll be able to give you all the pointers you need. Heck, it'll be so easy for you, you won't have to worry about it at all, will you, CE?"

Ray glanced back to find Cecil's eyes welled with tears and his lip in a pout as he reached out toward him.

"Had about enough of that stupid old wagon, did you?"

Dropping the handle, Ray walked back and swept his brother into his arms. He flung him around to one hip even though he didn't have the breadth in his hips to hold up a baby the way his mother did. She could carry Cecil around half the afternoon with him hanging on one hip. When Ray tried it, Cecil kept slipping down, forcing Ray to hoist him back up repeatedly. With all the slipping and hoisting, Cecil's tried patience wore plum through. Pretty soon he was hollering in Ray's ear. Large wet tears were sliding down his cheeks.

"If you're going to holler like a baby, then I'll sit you back down in that wagon, I swear I will."

When his hollers didn't let up, Ray sighed and dropped the wagon's handle once again. "Gawl dang it, Cecil. At this pace, it'll be midnight 'fore we get back. I told Mom I didn't want to bring you."

Cecil began kicking and squirming as Ray attempted to settle him back in.

"You're trying my patience something fierce, you know that?"

When it became clear to him that Cecil just wasn't willing to sit the bumps and jostles of the wagon any longer, Ray switched tactics and lifted his flailing brother onto his shoulders. His angry wails turned to giggles immediately.

Reaching awkwardly down to pick up the handle, Ray determined to finish off the final few miles into town as quickly as he could.

6

A Cold Storm

The wind was chill and biting when they arrived in the heart of Chicot. As his mother had instructed, Ray bought Cecil's medicine first then headed over to the mercantile for the beans and flour. There was a bench inside, and Ray sat there with Cecil a good while, finishing off the dried jerky and biscuits his mother had packed for the journey.

"If you promise to be good all the way back, I'll buy you a few lemon drops." Ray knew the bribe was pointless since Cecil didn't know yet what lemon drops tasted like, but he fiercely hoped there'd be enough money left over to buy a few. Ray loved the way they pulled at the inside of your cheeks, making them sting in a queer way.

Beside him, Cecil's eyelids were growing heavy.

"With any luck, you'll sleep the whole way back. I just wish Mom had sent along a blanket. With the sun hiding and the wind up like it is, it feels like February again, not March."

Spying a movement at the corner of his eye, Ray saw Martin Cowel, the owner of the mercantile, approaching.

"Well, I'll be. Ray Rowe. I haven't seen hide nor hair of your pappy for damn near the whole winter. How have you'uns been keeping yourselves?"

"It's been a long winter, sir. Cecil's been sick most of it, but he's on the mend now. Mostly my father's been buying our supplies straight off the wagon. I only came in today because Cecil's out of his medicine."

"You mean to tell me you walked all this way on foot?" Martin asked, rocking back on his heels and whistling. "And just the two of you? With a storm coming too?"

"I have the wagon," Ray replied, a hint of defensiveness in his tone. "When we set out, the sun was shining bright."

"There's a storm coming for sure. Winter's got to have her say a few more times before she retreats back up to the Arctic. My elbows and knees were as stiff as fence posts this morning. Anymore, I can about tell you as to the hour when a storm's gonna come. I expect this one will dump at least a few inches of snow before it's through too."

Feeling disheartened, Ray glanced out the window at the darkening sky. He suspected Mr. Cowel was right. With any luck, the snow would hold off until they were home.

"If I had an extra hand in the shop today, I'd give you a ride back to the river camp myself. I've got a few families who ain't been by in months to make payments on their accounts. I'll be out there in the next week or so to collect for certain."

Figuring there was no sense wasting any more time, Ray stood up and pulled Cecil into his arms. "My ma sent me for beans and flour, Mr. Cowel. Five pounds of each."

"Sure thing, Ray. We'll get you fixed up and on your way. And you can tell your parents that I'll be sure to pay them a visit when I make it out your way."

———◦◦◦◦◦———

To his frustration, Ray's boots seemed to be disintegrating more with every mile he walked. Fairly soon, there would be little difference between wearing them and not wearing them. Cecil woke up from the comatose nap he had fallen into upon departure with just three miles between them and the mercantile.

"Wish you could have slept on a few more miles, Ce. I don't relish hearing you wail in this bitter cold the rest of the way."

As if on cue, Cecil's halfhearted whimpers turned into loud, angry wails of protest. When a mixture of sleet, rain, and snow started spitting from the sky, his cries grew even louder. Every minute or two, a heavy bout of coughing would rake across his chest.

"You need this more than I do," Ray said, stopping long enough to strip his own tattered jacket off him and drape it around his brother.

His doing so seemed to help for what felt like a mile or two. Cecil stopped scream-crying and commenced to simply whimpering. The winds picked up, and pelts of sleet stung Ray's face like fire while he debated his options. He could seek shelter in a farmhouse if and when he came upon one. However, if he did, he knew his parents would worry something fearsome until they were home safe.

Besides, by the color in the clouds, Ray suspected it would turn to straight snow soon and would likely continue falling all night. Getting home tomorrow under clear skies but trudging along with the wagon through a foot of snow wouldn't be any easier than finishing the journey now. And it was almost always bitter cold for a few days after a storm like this one.

No, they needed to press on.

Ray paused only to readjust his soaked jacket over Cecil, who finally grew exhausted and chilled enough to consent to lie back down and allow the coat to cover him completely.

The sleet and snow blew sideways through the air, soaking through his shirt and trousers, and stinging his cheeks like fire. Without the jacket to shield the worst of it, Ray felt his strength fading, but he pressed the worry from his mind. All he could think about was getting them home and curling up in front of the woodstove.

He eventually stopped feeling and hearing and thinking and simply trudged on. He didn't even notice the variation of light on the road ahead of him until it was almost upon him. He felt the warm and welcome embrace of his father before he understood that his father had been traveling along the road to find them and was truly with them now.

Russell passed his coat to his son and draped a blanket over the whimpering Cecil. Then he took the wagon handle and threw an arm over Ray. "It ain't but another mile, Ray. We'll be back before you know it. I'm just sorry I wasn't home sooner to know you were gone. Your mother's in a mighty state with you two being stuck out here in this. A mighty state for sure."

In the dark calm of the tent, with the storm blowing wickedly outside, Ray felt he had never been happier to have the bodies of his brothers and sisters pressing in on him, welcoming him safely home. Only after his soaked clothes were stripped from him and he was toweled off did his chin begin to shake. He wondered if his teeth could withstand the force.

Katherine draped a blanket over him and curled up next to him on one side. On the other, he was tucked up as close to the woodstove as he could get without getting burnt. She kept beside him even though it meant her having to wipe the sweat from her brow every few minutes due to the heat the stove gave off. Ray's parents paced the room, trying to warm and revive Cecil, who was no longer crying at all. His eyes remained open as they carried him. They travelled over the objects in the tent as if in a daze.

Reluctantly, Ray choked down some broth even though he felt certain his stomach would refuse it. He only realized that he had dozed off with the mug still in his hand when he felt his body rock back and the warm liquid splash against his chest. Taking notice, his father pulled away from his mother and Cecil long enough to help him up to his cot and to throw a quilt over him.

"Sleep, Ray," he said, covering his forehead with his calloused palm in reassurance. "Things will be better in the morning."

Ray wanted to agree and to thank his father for coming for him, but he found his jaw to be too heavy and tight to do so. Instead, he turned to his side and closed his eyes. As soon as his lids were shut, it felt to him that he was back out in the storm again, cold and wet and pulling along a whimpering brother who was in no shape to be out in such weather.

He trudged through the snow all night in his dreams, ever lugging the rickety wagon along behind him.

It would prove to be the one nightmare he would have the rest of his life, walking helplessly through that storm, trying to get baby Cecil to safety.

<hr />

Ray woke to the brilliant light that only came after a heavy snow. It penetrated the tough canvas of the tent like a light straight from heaven. For a minute, he felt nothing at all. Remembered nothing. Then the horrible sound that had awoken him came again. Ray felt a sickening wave wash over him.

He had never before heard his mother sob like that, but in his heart of hearts, he knew without turning what it meant. A grief as powerful as that, escaping in those pitiful, half-suppressed sobs, could only have one meaning.

Forcing himself up, he scanned the tent until his eyes fell on his mother. She was sitting in a rickety chair, her shoulders shaking and tears flowing down her cheeks. Wrapped in a bundle in her arms was Cecil. His face was still, his eyes were closed, and his skin was a peculiar pale white-blue that Ray had never seen before.

Feeling his stomach rising into his throat, Ray dashed out of the tent into the blinding light and deep snow that covered the world. Clad only in long johns, he sank into the snow and dry heaved until his vision went gray. His stomach protested, telling him it had nothing at all to give.

His father arrived, kneeling down into the snow next to him and wiping the angry tears from his own cheeks. "There's something I want you to hear, son, and I want you to promise me you'll never forget it neither. I'm going to tell you it now, and we're not going to talk on it no more. Never again. Your mama won't be able to handle the thought of you harboring it, or any of us harboring it.

"You see, your mama ain't to blame for sending him along with you. You ain't to blame for agreeing to take him along. You ain't to blame for not getting him back here quicker than you were able to. And you ain't to blame for not stopping to find shelter elsewhere. Ain't no one to blame for this.

"I won't have you thinking you are, neither, so you're going to have to promise it to me now. You're going to have to keep it too because I might not have the strength to remind you of this again. God wanted our baby Cecil, and he took him. There ain't no more to be said than that. Do you hear me, son?"

Ray consented that he did, even as he felt a strange wall waking up to form a barrier around his heart. Nothing would be the same anymore. Not with Cecil gone. Nothing would be the same again.

The House behind the School

Emma and her family settled into their new lives with relative ease. Whether it was necessary for all roustabouts to come home turning things over in their minds the way her father did, Emma didn't know. But her father was always mumbling to himself and sketching on scraps of paper. Whenever she asked him what he was doing, he'd say he was figuring out the gin equipment. It seemed odd to Emma that her father could commit to memory such vivid images in his brain of the equipment that he could continue to tinker with it in his mind for hours into the night. But that is just what he did. It wasn't more than a few months that passed when she overheard him tell her mother that Mr. McCracken had announced that her father had the equipment working better than it had in years.

Emma's heart swelled with pride hearing this, even though it came as no surprise to her. If her father put his mind to it long enough, he could probably fix all the problems in the world.

Emma's mama got busy right quick making the shabby tenement house a suitable home. Before long, Emma and Billie Lee even had a set of pink gingham curtains hanging over their window. And somehow, buying as little as needed, her mama soon had all she needed to cook up the meals that made Emma's father exclaim with delight when he walked in most evenings.

Emma found it natural and easy to get to know the other kids living in the McCracken tenement housing. Her early hunches had proven right. Boys were best to be avoided. They tended to carry slimy things, living and even dead, in their pockets. Add to that that after a few hours in the sun, boys radiated a smell that made Emma's nose prickle. And they never seemed to want to stop moving.

Girls, on the other hand, were cleaner and smelled better. A few of them, most especially the foreman's daughter, had a tendency to be bossy. When Emma refused to kowtow to her, they decided they were better off just not being friends.

The best part of Emma's world began when the new school opened up a month or so after the flood ended. It was peculiar at first, walking through the halls and into the gymnasium that she had slept in for so long. Where before there had only been white paint, shiny tile floors, and newness, now there were posters and pictures and chalkboards. When she walked up the stairs to the second floor—the same stairs that she had forever ago continued on up and out to the roof—Emma felt her cheeks flush with a suppressed excitement. If there was ever a fire, she would know just how to get everyone out safely.

She looked around school once or twice for the boy she had followed out to the roof that day. Then she remembered that he had told her he was leaving town to live on the banks of the river again. She shuddered at the thought of living by the river that was the monster that had claimed her home. Wouldn't that be something if one of her lost dolls washed up at his feet one day? Then, thinking of the boys living in the McCracken tenement housing with her, the boys whose pockets were always squirming with living things, Emma found herself wishing her dolls would keep floating down to the Gulf. If they were ever found, she hoped they were found by a girl in need of a soft companion. Not by a boy who might cut off their heads or give them some other horrible fate.

As far as school went, Emma figured it was one of the best places in the world to be. Emma's first grade teacher, Ms. Collins, was not only the prettiest woman Emma had ever seen, she was the smartest too. By the end of her first week of school, Emma knew with a certainty as keen as any she had ever felt that it was her life's calling to be a teacher.

When she told her father this news, he beamed with pride and told her that he could see her making a mighty fine teacher. Maggie wasn't as completely won over by the idea. Without entirely dismissing her, she pointed out that it would be a difficult task to run a household and raise a family while holding down a demanding teaching position. But Emma didn't care. The only boy worth marrying had already been taken by her mother. And, considering the constant neediness of Billie Lee, Emma wasn't entirely certain she wanted to have children.

Before Emma knew it, the days started slipping into one another so fast that she hardly had time to keep track of them. Attending school was her favorite activity. Even more so than playing outside with the other kids that lived on her tenement block. Possibly even more than the long walks she sometimes took with her father. When she walked along the halls of the school, she'd let her fingers trail along the painted concrete blocks that lined the halls and imagine herself teaching in those very rooms.

Emma was in the middle of her third grade year when the winds of change hit their family. Long since having proved his worth at the McCracken Cotton Gin, Emma's father had become invaluable there. He had also earned the deep respect of John McCracken. One night her father came home beaming ear to ear. He hinted at nothing, however, building on the suspense of his secret as the evening wore on. He waited until her mother was practically in a fit as she finished cooking the last of their dinner, then he swept her into his arms and danced with her through the small rooms of their tenement house. Suppressing a smile, Maggie struggled and urged him to set her down before he stumbled and they went flying into a wall.

"You'll never guess," Dick said when he consented. His breathing was heavy from the exertion, but his smile was still just as deep.

"No," Maggie said, pretending to be put off by his show as she straightened her apron. "Clearly I won't and you've no mind to tell me, so I'm likely to go crazy."

"What is it, Daddy?" Emma begged, tugging on his arm until he hoisted her in the air up over his head then set her down and turned to his wife once again.

"Maggie, my dear, what would you say if I told you you're finally going to have a house to call your own? And a new one at that."

Maggie's face went white with shock, and her jaw dropped. "Dick, if you're fooling me, I swear, I'll—"

"Maggie, do I ever fool you?"

"Yes. Every day in fact."

"Well, not today."

"I—I don't see how it's possible. We haven't managed to save more than a few weeks' worth of pay in three years. We haven't the money saved to buy even a few windows, much less a door or a few boards."

"No, we don't. You're right at that. But John McCracken does. Hell, he probably has enough saved to buy a hundred houses. But the only thing that matters is that he intends to loan me enough so that we can build our own. It's even been decided where we can build it."

"Oh, don't keep us in suspense. Where, Dick?"

"Right behind that school of yours, Emma Jo. Just right there at that."

Emma felt a tingle all the way down to her toes. A real house of their own. And right behind the school. *Her* school. Not only was her school the biggest building in town, it was also the stateliest. With its bright red bricks in orderly rows, the school house had its own air of authority and nobility.

"How far from the school is it, Papa?"

"Well, its backyard will be in clear view of the playground, for sure. You'll never again want for a swing, Emma."

Emma thought of the massive oaks that covered the playground and shaded it from the scorching heat of summer. She had always felt a connection to the building, ever since the first night she spent in it. Now that connection was strengthening.

"It's that feat you pulled last month with them blueprints, isn't it?" Maggie asked, brushing large, wet tears from under her lids.

"He didn't say, but I believe it is."

Maggie wrapped herself around her husband and cried into his neck until the smell of burning chicken filled the house. She collected herself and made a dash for the pan, pulling it from the burner.

Emma turned to her sister, who had finally finished whooping and hollering and running around the room. "Did you hear that Billie Lee? We're going to have a house of our own. A real house. And it's going to be right there behind the school in the best spot in the entire world. Ain't we the luckiest ever?"

Billie Lee squealed and shouted as her father lifted her up and pressed a dozen kisses into her neck. He winked at Emma as he did.

"You're right about that, Emma. The way I figure it, we're about as lucky as we can get."

⚬⚬⚬

At the time he said those words, just a few months before the stock market crash of 1929, Dick didn't figure how long he was going to have to rely on that luck to get his family by. Modest by nature, he never accounted the good fortune that helped his family survive the Great Depression as anything more to his credit than sheer luck. Dick downplayed his uncanny knowledge of engines and machines and attributed it to the few years he had spent at the General Motors plant in St. Louis.

By the time the house was completed, the terrible shock wave of depression was just beginning to sweep through America. It struck in random bursts those first years. The market had crashed and didn't seem to want to recover. One bad harvest season turned into two. The rains that just five years ago had filled every nook and cranny surrounding the Mississippi for thousands of miles with water now made themselves scarce. The fields were dry. The crops were stunted. Sharecroppers were turned away by the dozens.

The new cotton gin equipment—equipment large enough to fill a gigantic warehouse—had been installed solely at the direction of Emma's father. Dick had spent days studying a set of complicated blue prints. When the equipment arrived, he was the only one in the entire plant who was able to understand them well enough to oversee its installation—something John McCracken had hailed as close to a miracle. Now in place and ready to go, the new gin was hungry for cotton. The little cotton that was harvested in the drought did nothing to task the operation of the massive gin.

A tension began to set up in her father as the seasons rolled by and conditions didn't improve. Friends by the dozens were laid off, lost their homes, or slipped away into the night to escape the call of debtors. Silently, Dick braced himself for the Depression to swing his way, to lay claim to his job, his home, or both. But it never did.

Although the promise didn't quite seem to reach his eyes, he assured his family on many occasions that his job was one of the safest at the gin. John McCracken had seen how instrumental he could be in repairing the massive equipment when it broke down. If something went wrong, Dick was the most likely one to manage the repairs time and again. So while his particular position was safe, one big fear was beginning to trouble him even more. He lay awake many nights nearly paralyzed with this fear. He fretted over it so often in fact that he began to worry that he'd bore a hole in the ceiling. Once the thought came to him, there was no quelling the rush of fear that accompanied it. It was the worry of what he'd do if the gin closed down entirely.

The home that he had built with money leant to him by McCracken was a modest one, an unassuming ranch with painted wood planks and a door that creaked when you opened it. Inside, there was a kitchen, family room, and three bedrooms. But modest or not, without the gin in operation, the Givens would most certainly lose everything.

Despite the poverty that raged through the Midwest, Dick's worries went unfounded. The gin stayed open, and he made enough money to feed and care for his family even during those hardest-hit years. When Maggie confided that she was pregnant with a third child during one of the hardest months he had seen, Dick tried not to let his belly seize up with fear. With the Lord's help, he had managed to provide for his family so far. His intentions were good and true, and he felt confident that the Lord would continue to favor him.

He thought of Emma, who at just over ten was fast growing into a young woman. He thought of Billie Lee, who was just three years behind, doing her best to follow in her sister's footsteps. God willing, he would do right by his girls.

As Maggie's belly grew, she kept busy calling on town folk suffering through harder times than they were. She and Emma and Billie Lee made certain to bake whatever extra they could and call upon those in need several times a week.

For Emma, as with most children, the fear of the Depression was more abstract than it was for her parents. For the most part, her life was unchanged, with the exception of the exodus of so many friends from East Prairie during those years. They kept their home, her father kept his job, and she and sister were busy with school.

Seeing the gaunt faces of the homeless men who had taken to sleeping in storefronts and parks did, however, give Emma nightmares. The hunger in their faces reminded her of the flood and how mother earth could take everything from you at such a short notice. The best way Emma could figure to fight a battle against her was to be smart and to get an education. With the same certainty that she knew the sun would rise each morning, Emma became even more certain that she was meant to be a teacher. Whatever catastrophes came their way, there would always be a need for teachers.

Once she was a teacher, Emma would never have to look into the mirror to find her cheeks gaunt and her eyes hollow and lifeless. Mother earth could play a mean game, but Emma was determined to be prepared to meet her with whatever the great mother sent her way.

8

A Wedge of Wood

The second time Ray kissed a girl it was behind a pawpaw tree at the back of the camp. Six painfully long months had passed, during which winter had given way to spring and spring had given way to summer. Now, in September, it felt like there was a whisper of autumn in the air.

This second kiss, like the first, was with Sarah. Unlike the first time, Ray no longer cared about awkwardness or about being at a loss for words. He had been at a loss for words for so many months that he figured he had no better chance of finding them now than he ever did.

He looked into Sarah's eyes when he pulled away—and he was the first to pull away—to find they were a muddy hazel color. It reminded him of the exact hue the Mississippi had been when he had stood on the roof of a school as a child to take in a flood that had nearly claimed the world all that time ago.

Perhaps registering his indifference, Sarah turned away and folded her arms. "I kept waiting for you to feel better," she said, clearing her throat. "And now we're leaving. I reckon you and me just ain't meant to be, huh?"

Ray yanked at one of the large, yellowed leaves of the pawpaw. In Sarah's mind, that kiss they shared the day his world fell apart cemented them together in some way. And even though he hadn't been busy talking to anyone, he still heard Sarah referred to around camp as his girl over and over.

"No, I reckon not."

"I was kind of hoping my pa would stay, and eventually, we could get married."

Ray started, but he did his best not to show it. He wondered what she would think if he told her that kissing her would forever remind him of terrible snowstorms and lost loved ones.

The words that left his lips were less painful ones to speak. "I'm afraid my family takes up about all I have to offer and I don't see that changing anytime soon."

"It was foolish to think it, I reckon. I just see how you are with your brothers and sisters. We all do."

"I hope...I hope you like California, Sarah. It should be sunny, from what I hear."

"It should be." She hugged him quickly then dashed off toward the wagon where her family's meager belongings were being loaded, but not before Ray saw the tears about to spill over her lids.

With the feel of her lips still uncomfortably on his, Ray took off toward the cemetery a mile or so this side of Chicot where little Cecil was buried. Alone, in good weather, and without the wagon, Ray could make the journey without even giving it a second thought.

It bothered Ray that Cecil was all alone there. Sure, the cemetery was packed full of other bodies. Other people's loved ones. Other babies. But there was no family there to comfort Cecil in his eternal sleep. His grave was off to itself and meagerly marked as if waiting for someone to come along and fix this injustice. Cecil hadn't lived long enough to make his own impact in the world, though he had certainly made it upon his family.

Ray knew not a day that went by that Cecil wasn't thought of and prayed for by every single member of his family. At mealtime, when the initial shock had worn off, it had become a habit of Ray's brothers and sisters to mention Cecil in some way, to bring him into conversation. Sometimes though, when Mary's shoulders were particularly slumped, they knew it best not to mention him aloud. Doing so on these days would just send their mother to bed early and full of unshed tears.

Upon arrival, Ray found the cemetery grounds full of blue asters. He plucked a few and laid them at Cecil's flat grave marker. He pulled a dusty lemon drop from his pocket and set it on top. He always saved them for him now. Every time he got one. If Cecil wasn't able to enjoy them, he shouldn't be able to either.

"I'd have bought less flour if I'd have known we didn't have enough money left to buy even a few that day. Or at least I wish that I'd have had the courage to ask for a few on credit when we didn't. I guess the prices go up as winter gets on and supplies dwindle. That's how come we were short on money. Mama didn't count on that part. I surely wish you could have tasted one, Cecil. The truth is, if we'd have had a magic looking glass, there's an awful lot of things we could have done differently about that day. I'm just sorry you were the one that suffered for it."

In the end, it was the monotonous routine of life that helped heal the Rowes' broken hearts. Words and prayers and well-wishes were not enough to mend the terrible ache that filled them in Cecil's absence. The passing of days, however, seemed to rectify them the most. Gradually, they became a functioning family of ten rather than eleven. This fact particularly troubled Ray because he had previously had an affinity for even numbers.

Regardless of how any of them cared for it, it seemed that life would continue on like this forever. Seasons slipped from one to the next, and Ray found himself growing into a man, whether or not he was ready to do so. His father commented that he would soon be strong enough to quit his schooling and join him on the banks of the river. The workdays, his father admitted, were long and tiring. But there was a peace in them, toiling away by the ancient and all-knowing river that was nearly as rewarding as the pay that he received.

Unwilling to complain to his father that this wasn't what he wanted, Ray braced himself for a day that would never come. In a way that Ray had never even dared to truly fear, their world was going to change again. And when it did, when it came to them unbidden and unwanted, this simple life by the river that he had known for so long would never be his again.

The morning that Ray's father died, there was no whisper of foreboding in the wind. There was no alarm in Ray's gut as he headed for the camp school with his siblings, chalkboards in hand. There was no particular premonition when he bid his father good-bye for the last time either.

Just as a villain, the morning offered no whisper of the events it held in store for them. It presented itself no different than a typical spring day. The rains had been heavy at times, and the riverbanks were a mess, but not in a way that was vastly different from any other spring on the Mississippi. There was no reason to believe that the brief but torrential downpour the previous evening would create conditions on the banks his father hadn't already met hundreds of times.

It was the late 1930s, and the great Depression was believed to be nearing an end. There was hope of recovery, of regrowth, and of opportunity.

When the foreman poked his head in to beckon Ray from class while he was in the midst of a complicated equation, it wasn't even noon yet. The particular fingers that summoned him out of the tent were long and crusted with the black soot of the river. His expression was grim and somber, exaggerating the deep lines that curved around his mouth.

"Hell, Ray," he said, gripping Ray's shoulder when he turned to face him. In doing so, he smeared the black soil of the swampy banks onto his shirt. "There ain't no good way to say this. There never is."

Ray felt a powerful numbness rushing over him as the foreman talked. He spoke in soft words of how his father's logging tractor had slipped on a wash of unstable earth while his father was hauling a massive trunk of a tree away from the dredging site. His father had acted on instinct, he said, to stop the slide down the embankment, but he had overcorrected the turn. The resulting force had created a momentum that sent the trunk, still secured to the grappling hooks and chains, straight into his father.

"Russell died quick, son. So quick he couldn't have felt any pain. You can seek comfort in that, if you can seek anything at times like these. We hope that such things will never happen, but against all hope and reason, sometimes they still do."

In numb oblivion, Ray felt himself being led home so that he could be present when the news was relayed to his mother. She needed to know that she wasn't alone, the foreman explained. She needed to be reminded that one of her sons had all but grown into a man and would be there to help her through these difficult times.

Ray stood silently to the side while the foreman and two other company men relayed the news to her. He felt a peculiar detachment watching her bear the news so stoically. She wouldn't break down in front of them. Neither would Ray.

"We're going to help you get on your feet," the foreman said, shifting uncomfortably and pinching the brim of his hat between his thumbs as he held it at his waist. "We'll get you set up in a nice town, find you a place to live, since you won't likely want to stay on here without Russell. We'll get you what money we can to get you started. Ray, you're a bright boy. Everyone says it. You'll be bringing in enough to compensate for your father in no time."

The three men took leave of them then. It was just Ray and his mother for a short interval before the school recessed for lunch and his siblings joined them. Joined them in knowing that their father was never going to walk through those loose tent flaps ever again. That his bright eyes would never gaze upon them and that they'd never feel his leathered hands assuredly squeezing the backs of their necks as was his habit.

In the men's absence, Ray found he could look anywhere but at his mother. In his peripheral vision, he noticed her squishing the front of her apron together over and over.

"He left his hat behind this morning, Ray. I thought I'd give it to him at lunch today. He gets such a terrible burn on his brow when he forgets it. That's all I could think when they were babbling on—how Russell forgot his hat this morning. I don't know why it bothers me so much, but it does."

Feeling the air escape from his lungs, Ray sank down onto a nearby chair. "It ain't supposed to be like this, Mama. If it weren't for the looks on their faces, I'd have hoped it was a prank of some sort. I expect—I expect I should go down there—where it happened. I expect if I don't, I'll never really believe it."

"Stay with me for now, Ray. If you leave me alone, I'll likely break down. I can't afford to break down like I did with…like I did before. You can't afford to either, I'm afraid. Your father would want us to pick up his strength and carry on. All your brothers and sisters are going to be depending on it for certain."

Ray brushed his thumb and forefinger over his brow as if he had a headache, when in fact he could feel nothing aside from a great numbness washing more deeply over him. "They'll be here any minute for sure. We were just minutes away from breaking for lunch."

"They're going to need comforting, Ray. If you could find it in you to give it, just for this afternoon, I'd be grateful. I'm afraid I haven't the strength to give any comfort today if I can help it. I'll finish getting lunch ready and see to it my babies have food in their bellies. We none of us can afford losing our strength. We'll be needing it for the road ahead."

<hr>

By the time his siblings were finished being alerted to the tragedy that had befallen their father and their family, Ray felt as if he were watching everything from a great distance. In his mind's eye, he saw himself passing out empty comfort where it was needed. His face looked surprisingly pale and gaunt and considerably aged.

Tears were shed in multitude, but not by Ray or Mary. They would each need to find their own private time to mourn Russell's passing. This, however, was not it.

After the long afternoon finally wore away into evening, Ray escaped down to the place on the riverbank where his father had been working. As was to be expected, work had ended early for the day. The mood in all of camp, as Ray had left it, had been decidedly somber.

Surveying the scene, Ray found that his father's body had been taken away. However, the tractor he had been operating had not. It had slid down into the black mess of earth where it would be stuck until the earth dried out. Ray crossed through the muck, his tattered boots making violent sucking sounds as he did. While his father's body was gone, the remains of the tragedy had not yet vanished. Red-brown blood littered the cab, causing Ray's stomach to lurch violently. A tree trunk nearly the size of the tractor itself was still entangled in chains and hooks at the tractor's front.

Turning from the blood-covered cab, Ray headed for the discarded trunk. He found himself wondering where it would end up eventually. It was just a worthless trunk of a tree, but it had taken his father's life. Ray found himself hoping it would be turned into something permanent and useful before it was over.

Pulling a knife from his pocket, Ray sawed away at the base cautiously until a large wedge broke off in his hand. *Fresh-cut wood has such a peculiar smell*, Ray thought. He turned it over in his hand a few times before holding it up to his nose. Since it was just a trunk, Ray no longer knew what type of tree it had once been. An oak, perhaps. Or a hickory. Whatever it had been, it had existed on this planet for many more decades than his father, based on its enormous bulk.

The sun was beginning to sink low on the horizon as Ray tucked his knife back into his pocket and began to forcibly work his way inland and out of the muck to the drier part of the forest. He turned the wedge of wood over in his fingers as he walked, knowing—but without quite being sure why— that he would keep it for the rest of his life.

9

A New Beginning

Perhaps it was due to the fact that it was only his second time on a train, but Ray kept thinking back to his first train ride even though it had been a lifetime ago. What a coincidence, he thought, that a decade and two losses of life later, he was returning to the very town he had departed from.

He hadn't expected to see East Prairie again. His family had no particular claim to it. No roots or ties in any way. It was just a town not too far from the river where his father had worked before the great flood inundated it, and it was only a few hours from where they had been staked at the time of his father's death. Now it was going to be his home. Without the need to pull up the stakes every so often and meander along the river as the need for dredging and reclaiming necessitated, Ray didn't see them leaving East Prairie anytime soon either. So long as they could find work, it would suffice as well as any other town. It was a peculiar feeling for him, as if fate was knocking on his door, whispering from the outside even though he refused to open it. *Hello, Ray. Welcome to your new home.*

True to their word, the foremen had covered the burial expenses for his father. They had also seen to the rental of a duplex in East Prairie through a connection of theirs. They were paying the Rowes enough money so that they could get back on their feet. Regardless of this, both Ray and his mother would have to find work, and quickly too.

They were going to live in a house, a shabby one quite possibly, but it would still be a permanent structure with solid walls and a roof. It would also have electricity. It was a very different life ahead of them. The only certainty they had was that they would have to work to keep it. When the meager payoff they had been given was gone, there would be nothing else coming except what they could earn themselves.

Ray felt with great certainty that his mother would never consider remarrying. She would work her fingers to the bone before she ever allowed another man to step into the void that his father left. The love they had shared ran too deep. Over the years, they had become a part of one another. The same way the hickories grew into barbed wire when a fence line was placed too close to them. After a while, the tree would encompass the wire, and the bark would seal over. They could no longer be separated without severely weakening or killing the tree.

That's how it was with his mama. His father was too much a part of her for her to ever let him go. He would always be there with them in a sense, even though he had parted from the living world.

As the train rocked steadily underneath him, Ray fought off a doze; but the urge was strong, and he slipped in and out of one several times. As always, now when he awoke, there were a few split seconds when he remembered nothing. His body didn't necessarily feel at peace in those seconds. He had never found peace since that day in the snow with Cecil. The calmness that he felt at certain times eluded him as soon as the memory of his father's death returned.

Like a bat swooping down over his head for a low-flying mosquito, the knowledge rushed back predictably as Ray pulled fully out of his doze once more and opened his eyes. He brushed the sleep from their corners and sighed. He fixed his gaze out the window and attempted to ignore the bickering of the twins who were fighting over a pencil that had rolled their way under the seats.

"What do you two want a pencil for anyway?" Ray asked when their bickering reached such a crescendo that unfamiliar heads were turning their way. "You haven't got any paper to use it."

"I can twirl it between my fingers, like so," Art said, demonstrating. His tongue stuck out in determination as he attempted to weave it between them. On the third half revolution, he fumbled, and the pencil went sailing under the seats again.

Protesting, Don punched his twin in the shoulder.

"Leave it be," Ray said, grabbing Art's arm as he attempted to rise from his seat.

Art's face flashed in anger. "Who died and made you…" His eyes opened wide at his blunder, and his cheeks flushed in shame. He stopped short and pressed his lips shut.

"Everyone says you're as smart as a whip, Art," Ray replied, feeling his stomach tighten into a knot. "I think you can figure that out."

Don twisted in his seat, looking across the aisle, while Art stared shamefacedly at his lap. His mother was sitting next to Katherine, who was younger than Ray by only a year. Her eyes were closed, and it didn't appear that she had heard the exchange.

"It's just boring, is all," Art said once he had summoned the words.

"Just try to sit still, will you?" Ray asked, having dropped the edge from his voice. "It won't be much longer now."

The twins settled down to finish the journey into East Prairie in a more subdued fashion. When the train slowed to a stop, Ray found himself glancing around for his father as he made his way to the luggage rack. Swallowing hard, he beckoned Earl, who was ten, to help hoist the loaded-down trunk. Katherine and Lucille, fourteen and twelve, grabbed the raggedy suitcases neighbors had passed on to them for the journey. Mary herded the rest of the children off the train after picking up what remained in a few crates.

There were nine Rowes altogether now. Nine Rowes and less than nine pieces of luggage counted for all that they owned. The majority of their belongings and furniture—the chairs, stove, table, cupboard, and tent had been left behind. The cots had been shipped up the day before they departed. They had been told that the house would be furnished sufficiently to get them started.

Ray had read enough about gypsies to feel like one as they made their way across town to their new home. He suspected word of their arrival and of their tragedy was already spreading by the long looks, whispers, and even the well-wishes they were given as they walked past storefront after storefront. The trunk was heavy, but pride kept Ray from relinquishing his grip and resting as they progressed.

On the other side of it, Earl took turns with Katherine, Lucille, and their mother.

"Looks like word of our coming is already making its way around town," Katherine said after Mary accepted another welcome from an older woman sweeping off the stoop of her home.

"News of misfortune spreads like wildfire, Katherine. It always does," Mary replied.

Ray surveyed the surroundings as they passed. He didn't have to know East Prairie from a hole in the wall to know that they were leaving the desirable side of town behind. The houses they were passing now were little better than shacks. Many weren't painted. Most of the ones that were had paint peeling off in strips in places. It seemed the majority of them were decently kept. A handful even had flower boxes in the windows. A few shacks—unkempt and falling into disarray—offset the nicer ones they passed.

Prior to the Depression, Ray felt it was likely that even this side of town would have felt above the reach of his family. Still, Ray had no misconceptions of how hard he was going to have to work to keep them living here while the nation was in such a depressed state. To keep a roof over their heads, food in their mouths, and clothes on their bodies. And shoes. Living in town, they wouldn't be able to go without shoes.

No matter how much Ray hadn't felt that life on the river was his calling, a tightness akin to claustrophobia started crawling up his neck. He didn't like the idea of knowing there would be people filling up his view at every turn.

"Just one or two more," Mary said, glancing at the addresses on the houses they passed.

"That's it there," Ray replied, having spotted the address in the doorway.

It stood out no differently than the others. It was a shotgun duplex. Rather than fighting the elements seeping through the canvas of the tent, they'd be sharing a wall with whoever owned the other half.

Mary pulled out the key from her pocketbook and passed it to Ray, who suddenly felt like he was floating after setting the trunk down on the porch.

"You unlock it, Ray. You're the man of the house now."

Ray obliged her even though he had no desire to. As soon as the temperamental lock gave way, the door swung open, and the twins pressed past him on both sides, whooping and hollering loud enough to draw neighbors to their windows.

"Well, look at this. It reminds me of nothing but a wide hallway," Virgie said. She stretched out her arms and walked from one room, into the next, and then into the third. The youngest aside from the twins, Virgie had often been called the prettiest of all the Rowe girls. Everything about her mannerisms, from the way she held herself to the way she moved, reaffirmed it.

"They call it shotgun housing," Katherine said, a defensive edge in her voice.

"Because a bullet can go straight through the front window out to the back," Earl finished for her, raising his arms in a mock shot.

The duplex consisted of three small, square rooms in total. Surveying it, Ray suspected the tent he had lived in all his life had been just as large, if not more so. The first room was the living room. It was stark and empty in its lack of furniture. The second room was packed tight with the cots that had arrived ahead of them. It would be used for sleeping and storing clothes. With all the cots in place, there wasn't a hint of floor space left for anything else. The third room was a kitchen, complete with a wood burning stove, an icebox, and a small table with four spindly chairs.

"I call this chair," Don said, plopping down.

"There's nine of us and four chairs. You will do no such thing," Mary reprimanded him. "We'll secure some more crates right quick, and they'll do fine until we can afford more chairs."

"There's a back porch at least," Ray said, unlocking the door and stepping out onto it. It had a pump and a sink for washing dishes and doing laundry. It looked out over a small yard into an alley.

"Look at that," Mary said. "I reckon I can do a heap of laundry in a sink that big. That's one thing, isn't it?"

"Not only that, Mama, but you missed the best thing of all. There's a real water closet in the corner of the bedroom with a sink and a toilet," Lucille exclaimed. "Imagine not having to use an outhouse. Don't that beat all?"

"I reckon we'll get used to that right quick," Katherine agreed.

Rather than following his siblings inside to inspect the flush toilet, Ray studied the yard in silence. His throat was tight and dry. He wanted to find his old cot and curl up on it under a heavy blanket. He wanted to hide from the sun, from noise and commotion, from his siblings, and from his responsibilities. He wanted to sleep. But there was unpacking to do and groceries to secure. And once they were settled, there were jobs to find in the midst of a heavy Depression that wasn't allowing much opportunity to land one. No, this was no time for sleeping.

Swallowing back unshed tears, Ray turned his back on the quiet yard and headed inside amidst a wave of commotion and the flushing of water. Perhaps, he thought, there might be time for mourning later.

10

Man of the House

For several minutes, Ray rolled the unfiltered Camel between his thumb and forefinger. The quiet blackness of midnight blanketed him. He sat on the porch in one of the chairs he had pulled from the kitchen after the crowded duplex had filled with deep, even breathing from the still bodies crowded within it.

Unlit, the tobacco smelled sweet and earthy. It smelled of his father. Without making a conscious decision to light it, Ray did so. The singe of ignited sulfur burnt his nostrils. The smoke and embers chased away the lingering sweetness of the unlit cigarette, creating the more familiar smell of burning tobacco that Ray associated with them.

He raised it to his lips and pulled in a regulated breath of air. He tried to hold that first breath in the way his father did, but smoke filled every corner of his lungs. His lungs seized up in protest. Eyes watering, he coughed in short bursts for a full minute then he tried again.

It got easier the more he tried it. By the time the cigarette was down to the nub, Ray thought he had sufficiently mastered the slow drag and calculated exhale he had memorized from watching his father smoke over the years. His lungs had stopped protesting as much too.

Ray was the man of the house now. His body seemed to be in a race to change as fast as his life. Not more than a few days could pass by before he had the need to shave a thick stubble off his face. His shoulders, chest, and back were thickening right out of every shirt he owned. Sometimes even he didn't recognize the sound of his own voice when he spoke.

Now, life was calling for him to pack away whatever childish notions desired to cling to him. His mother—and everyone else—expected him to be the man of the house, and he intended to rise to the occasion. He would attempt the daunting task of holding down as many hours at whatever job he could find, all the while finishing school when it resumed in the fall.

It had always been relatively easy for him to be a good student and do well in school, but the idea of attending school in East Prairie frightened him. It would be far different here. No longer would his classroom have the open air and freedom that came with the camp tent schools he had grown up with. The school here would have brick walls and overhead lights, a lunch room, and a gymnasium. Long hallways with bells and clocks, not the trajectory of the sun overhead, would proclaim the passage of time, another reminder of the separation from his father and the river life.

He had only been in a true school once in life, and at the time, he believed it had been enough. He had felt very much like his father in that crowded schoolhouse, packed with all those other families while waiting for the water to recede. He had wanted space, the earth, and the river.

Ray recognized the feel of fear tugging at his midsection. He didn't feel it often, but he had felt it enough to be familiar with it. It wasn't taking over as man of the house or holding down a job that turned his stomach. It was joining in with other kids his age in a real high school. He wondered if he was smart enough to make the grade here. On the river, he and Katherine had always been considered the smartest kids in camp. He was a natural at math. A few years prior, Ray had progressed to a point where the camp teachers could no longer teach him the subject. Now he joined in tutoring others during math time. He was a voracious reader too, whenever there had been books in camp to read. The problem with books was that they never lasted long enough. Ray would devour them and be left hungry for more, but none were to be had.

Here, it would be different. East Prairie had a library. So too, most likely, would the high school. Whether or not he had the time to read them any longer, all the books he could want would be available to him. That was the fear tugging at him. That while he was more than smart enough to fit in on the river, would he be smart enough to fit in here?

Ray did his best to shrug it off. If he wasn't smart enough, he always had his fists to rely on. He would manage. He could endure. Losing Cecil and his father had changed him. It was still changing him. He used to lie awake on his cot and let his mind wander anywhere it wanted to go. Now, when his thoughts started to take off, he reined them back in. A wild imagination and false hopes of a bright and promising future had no place for him in this world. He would finish school only because his father had dreamed he would. Being the first in his family to earn a high school diploma had been a powerful wish of his father's. And it was the final gift Ray wanted to give him.

Ray determined that he would get his diploma right along with whatever humiliation and hardship he had to endure in order to do so. What exactly he would do with a diploma, he had no idea. Those kinds of hopes for his future felt meaningless now.

Taking one last, perfectly executed drag on the cigarette, Ray squashed the nub onto the bottom of one of his father's work boots. He had taken to wearing them even though they were still a few sizes too big. It certainly beat going barefoot.

As he stood up, he felt a wave of nausea wash over him. The tobacco and nicotine had given him a dull, humming buzz that had started minutes ago. But now it was setting off an alarm in his body. He stumbled over to the base of a spindly tree and vomited. When he stood back up, his head was pounding. Wiping his mouth, Ray swallowed back another rush of nausea and headed inside. After swishing down a few gulps of cool, clear water from the porch pump, he collapsed onto his cot without bothering to shed his clothes or boots.

He closed his eyes and started to give in to sleep immediately. As he did, he pictured his father walking up to him out of the snowstorm and coming to his rescue. What would he give for his father to come to his rescue now? To throw his coat over him and tell him it was all right. That he didn't need to bear the weight of the world on his shoulders. At least until they were a little broader, a little stronger.

But his father wasn't coming this time. He was never coming again. A single tear slid out from Ray's closed lids and dropped down onto his pillow. More threatened to follow, but he forced them back. Nauseated and filled with a deep and powerful sorrow, Ray allowed himself to be lulled to sleep listening to the chorus of varied breathing that filled the packed, humid room. Maybe when he woke up he would be lucky enough to feel a little less. Maybe doing so would be enough to get him by.

⁓

When the Rowes arrived in East Prairie, there was just a week left before the school let out for the summer. To the delight of some of the Rowe children and disappointment of the rest, they would need to pass the coming summer before enrolling. Although learning had been different in the tent school, Ray's studies placed him somewhere between a sophomore and junior level, and Katherine wasn't far behind him. Lucille would study hard the coming months and attempt to pass into her freshman year. The rest of the children, from Earl down to Art and Don, would attend the very elementary school that had once sheltered their family.

The sun was up high overhead, and sweat was dripping down between Ray's shoulder blades when he passed in front of the high school the third day after his arrival in town. A piercing bell had rung from inside the towering building when he was still a block away. As he passed it now, in the windows he could see bodies packed together, milling about the halls like ants. While he was still in sight of them, the halls rapidly thinned to nothing. Seconds later, another bell rang. Ray felt his stomach ball up with tension as he wondered if he could do it. If he could blend in unnoticed and come out a few years later with a diploma. He also wondered if he should just scrap the hope entirely and set his sights on a full-time job. His father would never know. Besides, plenty of kids his age dropped out. Especially kids living on his side of the tracks.

Unfortunately, as the previous two days had shown, finding a job wasn't that easy right now either. It was his third day soliciting himself to just about anyone he could come across. He had never before thought of seeking employment as soliciting, but that was how several of the shopkeepers had phrased their rejections—no solicitation— human or otherwise. And the phrase had stuck with him. In his mind, solicitors were much like the carpetbaggers of the old days. *Oh well*, he thought, *being a solicitor was better than being a beggar.*

He had been in and out of dozens of shops and businesses. Most weren't hiring at all. A few were, but they found him too young and inexperienced to meet their needs.

With sweat dripping like a faucet now, Ray pressed on, stopping at water fountains along the way.

He paused in the shade of the IGA grocery store. Concrete blocks kept the glass entry doors propped wide open. The smell of fresh bread spilled out, mixing with the ripe tomatoes, cucumbers, and berries on display outside. Ray felt his stomach flip in hunger.

It was one of the last businesses in town that he hadn't approached. However, there was a sign in the window that very clearly stated they weren't hiring. Finally, deciding to pretend he hadn't seen it, Ray slipped inside and scanned the mostly empty store until his gaze landed on an older man whom he reckoned to be the manager, based on his dress and general look of superiority. Ray paused behind him expectantly, but he seemed preoccupied in straightening a display of canned beans.

"What are you selling?" the shrewd man asked as Ray cleared his throat in hopes of getting his attention.

"Nothing, sir," Ray replied. "In fact, I'm looking for a job. I'm willing to help out any way that you need. I'm strong, and I don't tire easily. And I won't require the same pay as some who might come your way." He knew he was selling himself short to advertise this, but he was through holding out hopes of acquiring anything of big financial importance.

The owner barked out a laugh and turned to study him. His sour breath filled Ray's nostrils, and Ray had to work hard not to blink or step back. "Son, if you're seeking employment, then you're still a solicitor, ain't you? Didn't you see the sign on the door?"

"I saw it, sir. I don't see how I could be a solicitor, but you aren't the first to suggest such a thing."

"You may not be selling *things*, but you're selling yourself. And ain't hardly anything more expensive than a man."

Having faced enough rejection, Ray took a risk. "Maybe so, sir, but I reckon it's also a better return on your investment."

"How so?" The man set his hands on his hips and studied him.

"Well, there ain't nothing you could buy that could intentionally improve itself through the act of learning, except a pup maybe, but that kind of learning is a good deal more up to the owner, the way I see it. No, there really ain't nothing out there that can improve upon itself the way a person could. There really is no better investment. If you would be gracious enough to hire me, I'd be obliged to prove it to you."

"Why ain't you in school, boy? A calculating mind like yours ain't meant to be in a dropout's body."

"I'm new in town, sir. I intend to enroll come fall. There didn't seem too much sense in enrolling now for just a few days."

"Well, let's hope Principal Harty holds on to his hat at the likes of you."

Ray suspected this might be a bit of a compliment, but he wasn't sure. This was the most luck he'd had engaging a potential employer in conversation, so he pressed on.

"If you'd allow me, sir, I know I don't need to spell out the benefits of hiring the young, but there are many. For starters, I suspect that my wages would be less than a man's. This would tax your pocket less."

"True, but your experience would be less as well."

"Maybe so. I won't debate that. But my back, legs, and feet are strong. I won't tire easily, and I won't need half as many breaks. And then, sir, there's my learning curve. It's a quick one, I can assure you. It's like buying a green broke horse for practically nothing and hardly needing to invest a bit of time to get him to pull your plow. And considering that he's young, he's likely to pull it longer too."

The shop owner laughed again, bathing Ray's nostrils in sourness. "I reckon your timing is as good as your sense of persuasion. I'll consider giving you a week's trial. Old Bob's back has been seizing up, and he ain't been to work in four days. He's a personal friend, so I'll have to find something for him to do when he returns. In the meantime, you can take his place at half his pay."

"Yes, sir. Thank you, sir! I can promise that you won't be disappointed."

"Have you got a name, son, or should I just call you Solicitor?

"Ray. Ray Rowe, sir."

"I don't know any Rowes."

"As I mentioned, sir, that's because we just came to town. My mother and brothers and sisters. I'm fifteen and the oldest of…eight children. My father, he died working on the river a few weeks ago."

A flash of sympathy passed over the man's face. "That happens from time to time, and it's always a shame. I suspect your mama's coping?"

"Yes, sir."

"With a young man like you to help her along, I can see why."

"Would you like me to start today? I'd be obliged to do so."

"Don't you want to know my name? Or at least what I'm going to pay you?"

"Yes, sir. I'm hoping you will share both actually."

"Name's Paul Yans. You can call me Paul. As for your pay, you'll be wearing out your back and your feet for the meager price of thirty cents an hour. It ain't much, but its minimum wage, and if you won't take it, a dozen others will be by in the next few days that will."

"I'll take it, sir," Ray said, accepting his hand and shaking it vigorously.

"Tell you what, son. Come by tomorrow at 7:00 a.m. and be ready to be put to work."

Ray thanked him again and headed back for home on a cloud. He was passing the high school when the bell rang again. This time, rather than filling the halls, the numerous bodies spilled out of its doors and onto the lawn. A group of boys about Ray's age stepped onto the sidewalk a half-dozen feet ahead of him. One boy glanced in his direction for a second, but the rest didn't seem to notice him at all. They whispered and snickered and punched each other in the shoulders. It became apparent to Ray they were mumbling something about girls, but he couldn't be sure.

For a brief second, Ray thought about calling out to them, but he decided against it. There was likely to come a time again in his life for making friends and talking about girls. But right now was time for getting his family settled. And Ray committed to doing his part the best that he could.

11

The Buffoon

As the minutes ticked away, the low hum of excitement grew louder until finally, all semblance of a structured and organized classroom fell away. Mr. Witmer, A. L. Webb High's science teacher, finally dropped all attempts to regain the attention of his students. With twenty-three minutes left of the school year, he resigned himself to the idea that learning was officially over until school resumed in September.

Unable to suppress a fresh bout of laughter, Emma inclined her head toward her desk, allowing her thick mass of raven black hair to hide her. Beside her, her best friend in the world, Loranna, let what sounded like a genuine snort escape, sending the students closest to her into further gales of laughter.

Acknowledging a lost cause, Mr. Witmer threw up his hands in defeat. "Unless anyone wants lines or would fancy staying behind to give my blackboard a good scrubbing, I'd suggest you do your best to keep your voices from spilling out into the hallway. Otherwise, I'm through. You may pass the final twenty minutes of your sophomore year talking quietly amongst yourselves. You've been a tolerable bunch. When I see you in town this summer, which I will, I hope it isn't while you are up to no good."

Loranna leaned over and poked Emma in the shoulder. "That isn't fair at all, hoping we're not up to no good."

Emma laughed. "Why not?"

"Don't you think our definitions of no good are entirely different from his?"

"Hmm, you have a point." Emma slipped her notebook into her satchel and felt something small and moist smack against her arm. She turned toward the back of the room to see Donnie Summerton aiming a second spitball at her. "Aren't you ever going to grow up?" she snapped.

"Why don't you try to make me?" he said just before sending a second one her way. This one sailed across the air and somehow made it through the separated locks of her hair at the back of her neck and fell down the collar of her blouse.

Emma felt her cheeks grow hot from anger as she felt it roll down her back. "Let's hope you can run as fast as you spit, you big buffoon," she threatened.

"He's got it bad for you, Emma," Loranna whispered, risking a quick and almost envious glance back at the small group of boys in the corner. They snickered, and a few punched shoulders.

"I don't care if he does," Emma said. As surreptitiously as she could, she untucked her blouse at the small of her back, letting the spitball drop to her seat. "He really is just a big buffoon.

Twenty minutes and half a dozen spitballs later, the final bell of the year rang. Chaos erupted like fireworks in classrooms and quickly spilled out into the halls. Emma and Loranna fell into a swarm of bodies as they stepped out into the hall, all screaming and hollering and slapping walls to make sounds of thunder.

"And *you* want to be a teacher." Being a full half a foot shorter than Emma, Loranna had to tilt her head and scream to be heard by her friend over the din of noise.

"Not for high school kids," Emma retorted. "I wouldn't teach boys like Donnie for all the money in the world. Thank you, but elementary school will suit me just fine."

"We will continue to disagree there." Loranna, like most girls in East Prairie, had little aspiration to do more than continue in school until she had either a diploma or a husband. If the diploma came first, a suitable husband would just have to follow.

Exactly where Emma's insistence to have a career of her own came from, Loranna couldn't fathom. All the mothers they knew had their hands full tending a home and raising their own babies. How such a task could ever be done while holding down a teaching job just didn't seem fathomable to her.

Outside, freedom and sunshine were abundant, overshadowing the frustration Emma felt over the unintentional harnessing of Donnie's attention once again. It seemed that the more she tried to reject him, the harder he made ploys for her attention.

Donnie was arguably one of the most popular boys at A. L. Webb High. He played every sport there was, he was tall and broad-shouldered for fifteen, and Emma had heard that he had started shaving when he was just twelve.

But Donnie had been her friend forever, and she couldn't fathom him being anything else. On top of that, Emma knew Donnie well enough to know that someday he would want a wife, and not just any wife either. He would want a dutiful, childbearing wife who would keep his home fastidious and have dinner on his table whenever he came home.

Perhaps Emma would one day grow up and get married. The older she got, the less repulsive this idea seemed. And maybe she would have a baby or two. If she did, she would do it on her terms. None of those things would take precedence over her teaching. Not one of them.

"Loranna," Emma began, "how many loaves of bread and pots of soup do you think Billie and I helped my mama deliver these last five or so years?"

Loranna wrinkled her nose. "How would I know?"

"It's hundreds, I'd bet. You and I have both known dozens and dozens of families—sharecroppers and the likes—who suddenly found themselves smack-dab in the heart of this Depression and helpless as newborn babies. Without people like us, they'd have likely starved."

"What's Donnie being smart on you have to do with that?"

"I'm just making it clear to you once and for all why I will never, *ever* like him."

"Because you may have to bring his mama bread?"

Emma laughed. "No, silly. Because I'm going to make good and sure that such a thing never happens to me, that's why. If that flood ten years ago hadn't thrown my father into the path of John McCracken, he'd likely never have gotten the chance to prove himself working in the gin. If he had gone back to being a sharecropper, who knows what horrible fate would have befallen my family. We might have had to flee all the way to California and live in tent camps begging for work like those thousands of others they say are there hoping for a change of fortune."

"That'll never happen to you and me, Emma, no matter how bad it gets. And I overheard Donnie say he aims to be a mechanic."

"Then why don't *you* marry him?" Emma huffed.

A light frown passed over Loranna's face. "You're the best friend I've ever had, Emma, but sometimes you just don't get it."

"What do you mean?" Emma felt her defensive side waking up.

"I mean hardly anyone's looking at me when I'm sitting next to you."

Emma felt her cheeks flush. "I never said you had to sit next to me. Besides, plenty of boys have been looking at you. And any ones who haven't, well, that's their loss."

Loranna shook her head, her brown hair falling over her face. She pressed her lips flat to fight off a smile. "You always know what to say, don't you, Emma?"

As they turned down her street, Emma grabbed Loranna's hand. "Don't look, but there's a passel of them coming our way now. And Donnie's smack-dab in the middle. Want me to tell them you're taking offers for a summer beau?"

Loranna swatted Emma on the shoulder. "If you do, I swear I'll never forgive you."

"Come on, let's run, Loranna. I bet we can make it to my house long before they can catch up."

Loranna agreed, and the two girls took off toward the safety of Emma's house as fast as they could.

"Best. Summer. Ever." Loranna screamed as the wind whipped her hair about her face. Their feet pounded against the sidewalk as they ran.

Emma opened her mouth to shout out an agreement but found she was laughing too hard to do so. To keep it from banging into her hip, Emma clutched her satchel at her chest. She risked a glance backward and saw that the group of boys was halfheartedly chasing them. Emma suspected they would give up well before they made it to the safety of her house.

<hr />

Two days later, Emma was sitting under the shade of an oak tree in her backyard and sipping on lemonade. It was early in the day; the sun was uncomfortably hot. If it wasn't for a tickle of a breeze, Emma believed her dress might stick to her skin permanently.

Oblivious to the heat, her little brother had planted himself in a patch of sunlight as he pushed his truck on a small mound of dirt.

"You're going to pop like a tick if you don't get out of the sun, Richard," Emma warned.

Richard, who was ten years her junior, ignored her and continued to make *vrooming* sounds.

"That's fine by me. Only your cheeks are getting bright pink, and any minute, mama's going to come out here and yell at me for not taking better care of you."

Spotting a movement in her peripheral vision, Emma turned to find Donnie stepping out of the back door. She groaned inwardly and crossed her arms. "If you've come to shoot spitballs at me, you'd best be on your way."

"Shucks, Emma, you know I was just teasing you." Donnie's face burned as he shoved his hands into his pants pockets.

Donnie lived less than a block away. They had known each other since they were kids. When they were younger, they had played in each other's backyards often enough. Now they seldom saw one another outside of school.

"I know you didn't come by here to get help with your homework either, since school's done let out."

"You aren't going to let me get a word out edgewise, are you?"

"I don't often talk to boys who shoot soggy spitballs down the back of my dress."

He pulled out a chair and sank down across from her. "Come to think about it, I guess that wasn't very nice of me, was it?"

"No, it wasn't."

"Emma, I was wondering if…if you might want to go to a movie later or something?"

Emma's mouth fell open before she could collect herself and pull it shut. "I…Donnie…I…that is, I think Billie and I have to go on some errands for my mother."

Donnie rapped the table with his knuckles. "How about tomorrow then?"

"Well, you see, the thing is—"

"The thing is what, Emma? You've got your whole future decided, and you figure I don't fit into it?"

Emma's jaw dropped open at his directness. "That isn't very nice. But you and I have been friends since we were kids. When you aren't being a first-class jerk, that is. And the truth is one of my good friends is a bit sweet on you. And friends have to trust one another and be loyal, too."

"Who?" Donnie asked, furrowing his brows.

"I can't very well say now, can I?" The truth was Emma couldn't say with one hundred percent certainty, but she had a strong hunch that Loranna had been harboring feelings for Donnie for a while now.

"Loranna?"

Emma dropped his gaze in hopes of avoiding an answer. She studied her brother hard to avoid his gaze. Considering that Loranna was her best friend in the world, it wasn't such a lucky guess. "Richard, get in the shade with that truck, or I'll swat you on the hiney, I swear I will."

"Is it?" Donnie persisted.

"Why don't you ask her yourself if you're in such a hurry to get a girlfriend?" Emma retorted.

"Maybe I will." Donnie stood up hurriedly.

"Where're you going so fast? I can see my mama through the kitchen window pouring you a glass of lemonade."

Donnie headed over to Richard and leaned over, hoisting him effortlessly into the air by hooking his hands in the hollows of his armpits. Richard stiffened in protest and kept his legs crossed perfectly, not wanting to surrender his mound of dirt. Donnie then plopped him unceremoniously down in the shade of the oak.

When Richard attempted to head back to his mound, Donnie blocked him with his foot. "Look there, kid, them roots make a better obstacle course than that plain old mound of dirt."

His comment worked. Richard studied the tree roots with raised eyebrows. A few seconds later, he was *vrooming* his truck along their irregular paths in the shade.

"Thanks," Emma said.

"Just do me a favor and don't end up agreeing to go out with Harold, will ya?"

"What makes you think Harold is going to ask me on a date?" Emma asked, her cheeks suddenly flushing scarlet.

"Because he said so on the last day of school, that's why. Only he's the biggest jerk I know."

"What is it with all you boys suddenly in such a hurry to go on dates? Of course I won't go on a date with Harold." Emma shuddered in revulsion. "To me, he'll always be that boy at the third grade picnic who cut off that bullfrog's legs while it was still trying to hop away."

Donnie put his hand to his stomach and flinched. "I had forgotten all about that."

"Well, I didn't. And I never will."

"So you won't go out with him?" he asked as if in self-assurance.

"Donnie, if you'd like, you can tell every boy in our class—and I do mean every boy—that I'm not going out with anyone. That's that."

The back door thwacked shut. Maggie Givens had just stepped out with a tray of cookies and lemonade, offering Donnie a glass as she approached.

Donnie thanked her and chugged it down in a few gulps, then set it back on the tray. "Thanks, Mrs. Givens. Emma, I'll be seeing you around, I guess."

"At the movies from the sound of it," Emma said, smiling a little. "And Donnie, regardless of who you end up taking, you can always keep stopping by here next year if you have questions about homework."

Donnie's smile was sheepish as he glanced over at Maggie. "Mrs. Givens, you've got yourself a daughter who's a teacher, and she ain't even a junior yet."

Maggie laughed. "Donnie, I've had a daughter who was a teacher ever since she was in grade school. Just ask her siblings. Now, you tell your mother not to be a stranger. I haven't seen her outside of church since Christmas."

He agreed, and Emma and Maggie watched him go. He fell into a jog before he rounded the corner. As soon as he was gone, Maggie cast her daughter a sharp glance. "Why does it seem to me that was a little short for a social visit?"

"Because he asked me to the movies, and I turned him down, that's why."

"Now, Emma, why would you do that?" Maggie asked in disapproval. "He's handsome enough and polite too. And he comes from a good family. Wait a minute. Let me guess. He doesn't fit into your perfectly figured life plans?"

Emma pressed her lips shut to hide a smile. "What makes you think my turning him down had anything to do with my plans?"

"Because you are a planner to the core, my dear. You like order and neatness and bricks that line up in rows. If a boy comes along who doesn't fit into that structured neatness of yours, then God help him."

Emma giggled. "That makes me sound mean, Mama."

Maggie walked over and pressed a kiss to her daughter's temple. "There isn't a mean bone in your body, dear. You are the kindest child I know. And there's no need to make excuses for wanting your life to be just so. You have a gift, and your father and I hope to see you use it."

"Thank you, Mama."

"Now, since you ran away your first would-be suitor and you've nothing better to do, how about doing me a favor and going to the market? We're in need of a few things for dinner."

"Sure, only can I wait an hour or so? I think Donnie ran off to ask Loranna to the movies. I'd love to swing by and see if I can spot them."

Maggie laughed. "Well, there's certainly no love lost on your part, is there?"

"No, Mama, there isn't," Emma agreed.

"I can't wait to meet the boy that captures your heart, Emma. I suspect he'll be entirely different than the dozen or so who have already caught your sister's eye, different from all these East Prairie boys."

"Whoever he is, if he *is* at all, he won't be one to shoot spitballs at me to get my attention."

"You're for sure right about that," Maggie said, shaking her head.

Emma took a glass of lemonade for herself, and for a few minutes, she and her mother sat in the shade laughing at the general ridiculousness of young men.

12

A Reunion of Sorts

When Emma finally set off for the store, the soft, cooling breeze had abandoned her, leaving her feeling sticky, hot, and crabby. At the last minute, Billie had asked to come along, and with both girls set to be absent from the house for an hour or so, their mother asked that they tote Richard along as well. They had agreed begrudgingly.

Emma and Billie progressed through town toward the IGA in silence since the sun was so hot that it all but stole their words. Behind them, they pulled Richard in a red scratched-up Western Auto wagon.

It annoyed Emma to no end that Richard refused to sit on his behind when she asked him to. Instead, he sat on his heels and bounced at every opportunity, making it twice as hard to pull the wagon.

"You're going to fall out and land on your head, you know," Emma snapped. "And neither Billie nor I are going to feel sorry for you."

"That ain't so," he protested.

Whenever she wasn't paying attention, he made practice shots with his slingshot at whatever object he fancied—living or inanimate.

A group of older boys who had already graduated from high school crossed the street from the pharmacy and fell into step a dozen or so feet behind them. They were talking and laughing and most likely not paying the least bit of attention to Emma and her family. Still, Emma noticed Billie's face flush hot.

The way Emma saw it, Billie had two things going against her lately. The first was that her body was changing. As a result, she was suddenly becoming very self-conscious of her looks. She fretted over herself constantly. The second was that she had somehow or another taken to noticing boys. In Emma's opinion, these two facts combined made her decidedly less fun to be around.

Beside her, Billie cleared her throat uncomfortably and smoothed out the back of her dress repeatedly.

"What are you going on about?" Emma whispered. "Are you worried you sat in something? 'Cause your skirt is clean. I can see it from here."

"It's not my skirt, Emma. It's my legs. Can't you hear them laughing? Those boys behind us are laughing at my legs. It's horrible, I tell you. Horrible."

As nonchalantly as she could, Emma tried to make it look as if she was turning around to check on her brother while she did a quick study of the group of boys. There were four in all, and they didn't seem to be paying Billie or any of the three of them any attention whatsoever.

"Oh, pshaw, Billie, they aren't looking at us at all. Besides, why would they be looking at your legs? They're just as ordinary as anyone else's legs, from what I can tell."

"No, Emma, that's not true. My legs aren't like yours. They aren't like anyone's."

Emma's brows wrinkled into a knot as she studied her sister. "That's the strangest thing you've ever said, Billie."

Billie bit her lip, and Emma could tell she was on the verge of tears. Exasperated, Emma shook her head and tried to think of something to say that would take Billie's mind off her ridiculous notion.

"The sun is just scorching today, isn't it? I hope we have enough left over to buy a few soda pops."

Billie agreed but seemed to close herself off to further conversation. They traveled the rest of the way in near silence. Emma gave a sigh of relief when they finally made it to the shade of the IGA.

Richard popped out of the wagon and dashed inside while Emma was parking it on the sidewalk at the front of the store. He refused to heed Emma's demand that he stay with them. Forcing back her growing frustration and abandoning Richard to whatever fate awaited him inside, Emma pulled the short grocery list from her pocket. String beans, carrots, butter, rhubarb, and cream of tartar.

"Richard's lucky you had the forethought to pull the wagon into the shade, otherwise it'd be boiling hot when we got back," Billie said, coming out of her shell a little.

Emma and Billie kept together once inside, discussing quantities and cost, and trying to figure if they'd have enough left over for what they really wanted. Soda pops. Emma kept her eye open for Richard and spotted him a few times spying on them from the corners of the aisles. When she finally managed to get a hold of him, she was going to scold him and scold him good.

She had just put the carrots into the cart when a terrible crashing filled the otherwise quiet store. It was a discontinuous and erratic toppling sound that seemed to last forever. Cans, Emma realized. Her heart sank.

"Please, please, please don't let it be Richard," she mumbled as she headed for the source.

"Who are you kidding?" Billie asked, trailing along behind her. "We both know it is."

Emma rounded the corner of one of the far aisles to find an entire display of canned tomatoes crashed to the floor. She held her breath as she searched for Richard. For a moment, hope swelled. He was nowhere in sight. Then she spotted him peaking at her from behind an end cap two aisles down. His face was bright red in embarrassment. Feeling her anger rise, Emma motioned him over with her best "I-mean-business-and-I-mean-it-right-now" look.

Almost to her surprise, he ducked his head and shuffled toward her.

"Richard, did you do this?" she asked as he approached with his head down.

"I might have, but I can't say for sure. Them cans just sort of jumped out all of a sudden when I was passing by. I'm sorry, Emma."

"Jumped out, my foot," Emma retorted. "You get down on the floor right quick and help us set them back."

Richard nodded and sank to his knees immediately, knowing full well when his sister meant business. And she meant it right then.

"Boys! Don't they just beat all," Emma exclaimed, setting her hands on her hips and shaking her head adamantly. Her coal black locks bounced in the bright lights of the store as she did.

Just as Emma sank down to her knees to start picking up the many cans, a young man standing nearby caught her attention. She looked up at him. His eyes, which were focused entirely on her and not the dozens of cans scattered all around, were wide in disbelief. His lips were slightly parted as if he were seeing something that he couldn't quite believe he was seeing.

Emma tucked her skirt under her knees and sank back on her heels as she scooped up the cans closest to her. Uncomfortable holding his direct gaze, she glanced down at his shirt. There was an IGA name tag fastened to his shirt pocket. No wonder he was staring at her like that. He worked here.

"I'm sorry, sir," Emma said, realizing as soon as she said it that he was likely no older than she and therefore not worthy of being called a sir. "It was an accident."

Pulling out of his stupor, the boy shook his head and bent over immediately, grabbing a few cans in order to start restocking them. "It...it doesn't look like any of the cans are bent."

Emma noticed his flushed cheeks, dark skin, and thick, wavy hair and felt her own cheeks flush unexpectedly.

"Richard hates to sit still," she offered in apology. "And even more he hates to listen to his big sisters."

As she finished, Emma glanced over at Billie, who had neither spoken nor bent down to help with the cans. Instead, she stood there with her lips pressed together, awkwardly smoothing out the front of her dress. *Oh, Billie, enough with your legs,* Emma wanted to snap.

"I listen just fine," Richard protested, passing the boy the cans he had picked up to be reshelved.

"I hope we don't have to pay for any of these," Emma said, worrying about the cost of so many cans.

"You won't," the boy replied quickly. "They're not damaged," he added when she paused to look at him.

Emma faltered for something to say. The situation was embarrassing enough without the sting of silence. "I don't recognize you from school. Don't you go?"

"I'm new in town. I've just been here a few weeks. I aim to enroll come fall."

"Oh, what grade?"

"Junior, I think."

"Me too. I'm Emma. This is my sister, Billie. And you might as well get introduced to my brother. I'm pretty sure the entire town knows his name by now. This is my little brother, Richard, and somehow he manages to be just about at every place at once."

The boy smiled at the remark and nodded at Billie. "I'm Ray. I have two brothers about his age. However mischievous he is, I bet they could give him a run for his money."

"I reckon they'll go to school together then too. The elementary school is a wonderful place. I'm sure they'll love it."

"They will if they can sit still long enough," Ray agreed. "They are particular about their freedom. More so than any kids I've ever known."

Emma glanced up from gathering the cans and met his gaze, and for some reason, she felt an involuntary sharp intake of breath. There was something peculiar about him that she couldn't put her finger on. "You say you just got into town?" she repeated.

"Yes," he said, turning back almost guiltily to the display of tomatoes that he was rebuilding.

"Oh well," she said, passing him the last few cans. Their fingertips brushed against one another as he took them. Emma felt her chest constrict involuntarily. "It's a small enough town. I'm sure we'll be seeing you around."

Ray nodded and belatedly offered Emma a hand as she stood up. Emma took it, though she felt with great certainty that both their cheeks had reached their darkest shades of red by her doing so.

They parted ways, and Emma hurried to secure the rest of the items on her list without thinking much about them. Humbled for the moment, Richard stuck by her side and demonstrated a rare obedience. Emma knew the whole event had her frazzled, but she felt it with a greater certainty at the register. If it wasn't for Billie reminding her, she would have checked out without adding the soda pops they all three had been craving.

As soon as they were outside, Billie seemed to relax again and grabbed Emma's arm. "Emma, did you see his name tag?"

"I didn't read it. Why? He said his name was Ray."

"Yes, but I'm talking about his last name. Rowe. Didn't you hear Mother talking about the Rowes the other night at supper?"

Emma gasped as she picked up the wagon handle. "That's the boy whose father just died in that accident on the river then, isn't it? The one Mom was raving on about for so long?" Emma twisted back and attempted to steal another glance at him, but the glass windows were too reflective in the bright summer sunlight. "I hardly believe it. He just seemed like a regular kid, didn't he?"

Billie shrugged. "I thought he was mighty cute. From that scarlet blush you had, it seemed like you did too."

Emma ignored the comment and turned over in her head the things her mother had said about his family. Maggie had gone along with some of the ladies from their church to welcome the family and bring them food and some home furnishings that they would need to restart their life in East Prairie. Emma's mother had rambled on and on over the course of their dinner about the bravery the mother and eldest son demonstrated at the loss of their respective husband and father—the family's sole breadwinner. Maggie had been moved by the way they seemed to be accepting the responsibilities that came to them with their abruptly changed lives.

If Emma remembered correctly, they were living on the far side of town in a public housing project where nobody she knew ever wanted to be seen. Most of the kids from that side of town had already dropped out of school some years before.

A rush of relief passed over her as she realized she could have been introduced to that boy there and not here. "Oh, Billie, I'm so glad Mom went to visit them while we were still in school. That boy would likely have been horrified to have kids his own age offering his family handouts, especially considering we'll be in school together. I hope he doesn't realize Mom was with them."

"Look at you, worrying over something that didn't even happen," Billie said, smiling a little. They had popped the tops of their sodas while still inside. Billie lifted hers up and took a swig. "I knew it had to happen sooner or later."

"What had to happen?" Emma asked, enjoying the soda a bit less than she expected since she was so preoccupied.

"A boy actually turned your head, Emma Givens."

Emma waved her hand to dismiss the idea. "You're the one who made the connection, Billie. I didn't even notice the name on his name tag the way you did."

Billie grabbed her arm once more. "Of course you didn't. You couldn't have, Emma. You two were too busy making goo-goo eyes at each other to notice anything else."

Emma brushed off her sister's comment with a laugh although a small part of her felt the truth in her words. The peculiar encounter had left her more than a little befuddled. And she couldn't deny—at least to herself—that she had to resist the urge to crane her neck to look back at the store once more as they turned the corner in hopes of another glance at the new boy in town.

——————

There was a ball in the pit of Ray's stomach that felt like lead. His arms, chest, and legs, on the other hand, felt as if they were flowing with adrenaline. He practically held his breath as Mr. Yans paused behind him, studying his next restocking project over his shoulder.

"That's one thing I hate about summer," he said from behind Ray. "Kids running rampant in the store. You'll pick up your fair share of those messes 'fore school resumes. Mark my words."

Ray nodded and tucked his hands in his back pockets. "Do you know them, sir?"

"I manage the IGA, son. I know everyone in East Prairie. Work here long enough and you will too."

Ray frowned to himself at this answer. He was hoping to ask Emma's last name or if Paul knew anything about her, but this reply didn't necessarily lead him into doing so.

"Dick Givens is their pa," Mr. Vans continued to Ray's delight. "They're a good enough family, regardless of the spill. Old Dick's about as admired as anyone these days. He works at the cotton gin and can't do wrong by John McCracken. That fact is getting his family through this here Depression, that'll be sure."

Ray had to bite his lip to keep from asking more as Paul walked away and left him to stock the canned soup that had arrived on the morning truck. "Emma Givens," he said to himself almost silently in order to test the sound of her name. He liked it, just like he liked her bright blue eyes and her bouncy coal black hair.

It had been almost a decade since he had last seen her, but Ray couldn't mistake her for anyone else. No matter how much time had passed. Those few minutes locked on the roof with her when he had been so terribly afraid of heights had been enough to cement her face in his mind forever. Of course, she was grown into a woman now, or nearly so. But she still had the same determined look in her eyes and set of her chin, like she could take on the world if she chose to. "*Boys*," she had said, both then and now. As if by saying the word, they would make sense to her.

And she struck Ray as someone who wanted to know and understand the order of the universe. Boys and everything else she encountered right along with them. She was bright, surely. The sharp look in her eyes made it impossible to think otherwise. She was tall for a girl and thin too. Pretty enough to remember, pretty enough to draw the attention of boys all around, boys in situations far better than his. She was pretty enough not to need to associate with a kid who lived on the wrong side of town and had no time at all on his hands any longer. Soon enough not to take any notice of him whatsoever.

Ray sighed and tried to push her from his mind. He couldn't though. The bright blue of her eyes burned in his memory more clearly than the stark red labels on the cans of soup he was shelving.

There had been a split second when she had looked at him that Ray felt certain she would remember him as well. However, he hadn't been entirely sure he wanted her to. She had been the brave one that day, not Ray. All Ray had done was get them in a pickle and then freeze up in fear at the idea of being stuck up on the roof where no one would hear them.

No, he had decided when the flash of recognition had passed from her face. He was best off not reminding her of their brief connection. Some things were simply better off not spoken of. He decided right then and there that if he ever got the chance to display bravery around her again, he certainly wouldn't fail to do it.

"Emma Givens," Ray repeated to himself as he finished shelving the last few cans in the box. He stood up and wiped his hands on his back pockets, and then he grabbed the empty box and headed for the storage room. "Hope you come back real soon."

13

The Boy at the Store

The rain pounded on the roof of the stockroom, and thunder boomed across the sky and reverberated along the walls, making Ray feel as if he were in a tin box. A tin box or an oven. Sweat rolled down his back, soaking his shirt. It slipped down his temples and forehead and onto his shirt collar.

More than ever in his life, Ray was tired of summer. He was tired of the scorching heat and the humid and dank unrefrigerated stockroom that sucked the air out of his lungs as soon as he entered it. He was tired of twelve-hour days and mountains of new shipments that arrived as soon as old ones were unpacked.

When the storm was nearly passed, he headed out the back door to the parking lot and lit a cigarette. Lingering under the overhang, he glanced up at the dark sky that was beginning to brighten in the west, promising clear skies the remainder of the day. It was late afternoon, and steam was steadily rising off the pavement, causing the afternoon to feel even hotter.

George Lacy stood ten feet away in the parking lot, resting one foot in the doorframe of his 1934 Ford flatbed pickup, smoking and listening to the radio.

"You hear what happened over in Poland earlier today?" George asked.

Ray filled his lungs with a drag before replying that he hadn't. He didn't know anything about Poland, and he wasn't entirely sure he cared either. George was a sucker for the news.

"Damn German soldiers attacked with a vengeance. They're expecting Russia to jump in on the attack too. Just divvy it up and divide the spoils between them. Hell of a mess, I tell you. Mark my words, if this ain't just a baby step in a long procession of terror, I'll eat my brother's socks. They're saying France and England will declare war on Germany over this. We're in the crapper now." George took a drag on his cigarette then reached inside to flip his radio off. After slamming the truck door, he pointed his finger at Ray. "We're in it for sure. It's going to be some kind of dog fight, boy. You just watch."

Ray frowned. He wasn't much into politics and didn't spend his nights hovering around the radio listening to talk about tensions in Europe the way his mother did, but he knew in his gut that this was bad news for certain. Fearing an attack was entirely different than there actually being one. "It don't sound good, that's for certain."

"No, it don't."

The rain had all but subsided now. All that was left felt meager in comparison to the massive downpour of only minutes before. The thunderstorm had been quick and violent, the way late summer storms tended to be. Before long there would be nothing left of it aside from the humidity rising back off the ground, returning skyward.

Ignoring the lingering drips of rain tickling his shoulders, Ray stepped out from the shelter of the awning. Heat and steam were rising off the brick walls behind him just as strongly as they were off the ground, reminding him of an oven's interior.

When he finished his cigarette, Ray headed back inside. Unable to summon the energy to reenter the sweltering stockroom, Ray meandered up to the front of the store, hoping for an hour or so break at the register. He didn't mind the lonely stockrooms, and in summer, he welcomed the two refrigerated rooms. He liked the solitude and the consistency of the work that came with the hours spent in them. He enjoyed keeping busy, keeping his mind focused.

He typically spent the other half of his days working at the registers. As a result, whether he wanted to or not, Ray was quickly learning who was who in the town of East Prairie. He suspected Paul Yans was right. If he worked at the IGA long enough, he'd know everybody's business whether or not he cared to. The summer had gone by, and he hadn't made any friends, but that didn't bother him any. Thanks to his work at the IGA, he suspected he knew the faces of almost every kid that would be enrolled in A. L. Webb High when it began the following week. He didn't know all their names, but he had a fairly good idea of the kids he might be interested in hanging around with, right along with the kids he wouldn't be interested in spending much time with at all.

Most of the customers that frequented the store were his mother's age or older. They shopped to feed their families, and they shopped with direction and purpose. They filled their carts, and Ray helped them haul their bags to their cars. It was these purchases that provided the majority of the IGA's income.

However, plenty of kids his age came in through the day as well. Some were on errands for their parents. Others came in to buy things for themselves. They bought cigarettes, soda pops, Licorice Snaps, Chick-O-Sticks, 5th Avenues, and 3 Musketeers. The boys often hung out in the parking lot afterward. They smoked and flirted with any girl walking by. When the excitement dwindled, they left and meandered down to the theater or bowling alley in hopes of more action. Plenty of girls came in too. Only, rather than being openly flirtatious like the boys were to them, they'd hold their hands over their mouths and giggle. They giggled at everything. In particular, Ray felt they did a lot of giggling at him.

Ray would often pass groups of his future classmates on his way home. A few times, he had been tempted to join in the fun, but his workdays were often long at twelve hours. In addition, there was always something that needed his attention at home, something broken, stuck in a drain, lost, or in general need of repair.

He was fairly certain that not a single day had gone by that at least something was waiting for him to tend to before he got a chance to rest and eat the best meal his mother could make under the circumstances they found themselves in. Mary was busy with laundry—hers and others, which she took in to earn extra money—when she wasn't putting in hours of her own at the stave mill. Mary had been lucky enough to get a job there just a few days after they had turned Ray down. She didn't do much at the mill aside from keep the floors swept clean, but it amounted to food on the table all the same.

Day and night, Mary worked her fingers to the bone while Katherine and Lucille took over most of the duties of seeing to their siblings. With the exception of the twins, most of the Rowe children managed not to add undue stress to an already chaotic and challenged world. The twins always meant their best, but keeping still and out of harm's way was a skill that simply eluded them. Mary, Katherine, and Lucille seemed to resign themselves to this fact early on. God willing, the twins would prevail, regardless of their lack of ability to govern their energy.

Ray was running his fingers through his damp hair when he reached the front of the store. The lone customer standing at the counter with her back to him stopped his heart right in his throat. The way she was turned he couldn't see her face, but he recognized her immediately. Emma Givens. Her clothes and hair were wet, and there were goose bumps on her arms. As if sensing his approach, she turned toward him. Her eyes widened, and her cheeks flushed instantly. She didn't giggle like other girls. Even though he didn't know her very well, Ray suspected that sort of silliness was beneath her.

He had seen her twice more over the course of the summer, once in the store and once in a group of other kids as he was passing by the five-and-dime on his way home. They had not spoken on either occasion.

Now, speaking seemed unavoidable, and that suited Ray just fine. He doubted that a day had passed that he hadn't thought about her in some way or another. He turned first to Bob, who had returned to work a month prior after a long string of issues with his back. He wasn't up to much yet, aside from checking the groceries, and he needed breaks as often as a lazy tomcat.

"Want me to take over for you awhile, Bob?" Ray asked, trying to keep his voice calm and even in the presence of Emma.

Bob wasted no time taking him up on the offer. He told Emma that it had been nice talking to her and headed for the back of the store, rubbing the small of his back as he went.

With just Ray and Emma and no one waiting in line at the moment, Ray felt his pulse pound even quicker.

"Did you get stuck in the storm?" Ray regretted the question immediately. Her wet clothes and hair proved that she did. Most likely she wasn't the type of girl who liked boys who felt it was necessary to state the obvious.

"A bit," she replied, crossing her arms over her chest. "I weathered most of it in here, or I likely would have floated away or been struck by lightning. For a bit it looked like a river washing down the street."

Ray nodded and searched for something else to say.

"Did you get registered for school?" Emma asked him. Ray told himself not to believe it, but he would have sworn to the hopeful look in her eyes.

"I did," he said, tying on an apron and stepping behind the register for something to do. "I'll be a junior like I was hoping."

"Then we'll have classes together, I'm sure. The junior class isn't that big."

Ray nodded. He wanted to say that would be nice, but his throat suddenly wouldn't let him. Instead his gaze fell on the soda in her hand, and he blurted out the stupidest question he could think of before he was able to pull it back. "Did you pay for that already?" *Dumb, Ray, dumb.* It was open already and half-drunk.

Emma bit her lip. "Actually I didn't have any money on me. I was across town at a friend's. Bob gave it to me. He knows my father."

"Oh." Ray felt his cheeks burn in shame. Now it looked like he suspected her of thievery. "Are you cold?"

"Not so much anymore."

"Oh."

"Are you looking forward to school?" She seemed to be as eager to keep the conversation going as Ray, only she was doing a better job of it.

"Yeah, very much. Are you?"

"I am. I love school. I think I'm the only one of my friends who does, but that's probably why I want to be a teacher."

"I didn't know that." Of course he didn't. He didn't know anything about her at all really.

"I…um…I was wondering if you've met many people yet? I know some boys I could introduce you to. Ones from the football team even, if you want to play."

Ray felt stuck for an answer. Football and all the other things that went along with high school felt like a dream to him. He would never have time for it, even if he wanted to, which he wasn't sure that he did. The only thing he knew for certain was that he wanted to keep Emma talking. He liked the way her wet, black curls bounced when she moved her head. With her clothes wet and sticking to her, he had an almost overwhelming urge to wrap her in a hug. He would never act on it, but he couldn't get the idea out of his mind either.

"That would be swell," he agreed aloud. "I don't expect I'll have enough time on my hands for football though or much of anything else for that matter."

"Oh." Emma bit her lip and frowned. "That's right. I heard about, well, what your family's going through. If there's anything else you need—"

"Thanks for the offer. We're fine."

"Will you still work here once school starts?"

"Yeah, as much as I can."

Ray glanced behind Emma as an elderly woman shuffled her way to the register. Emma stepped back hesitantly.

"I should go."

Ray felt his throat close up again as the customer started setting cans and a bag of apples on the counter in front of him. Why couldn't he think of anything worthwhile to say to her before she disappeared?

"Did you hear about Poland?" Ray blurted out.

Emma nodded. "My mother's been listening to the radio all day." She turned and headed for the door. "I guess I'll see you in school then."

"Do you need an umbrella?"

Emma shook her head. "It's not raining anymore."

Ray found himself reaching automatically for a can on the counter in front of him when what he really wanted to do was jog out the door after her. He did his best to suppress a groan of frustration.

He looked her way helplessly. Her hand was on the door, and she had turned away from him. One foot was over the threshold when a few more words finally came to him.

"Good-bye, Emma Givens."

Her head whipped his way in surprise, and her cheeks flushed crimson. "Good-bye, Ray. I'll be seeing you."

The old woman in front of him cleared her throat before Emma was even halfway across the parking lot. The action startled Ray back to reality.

"It gets easier," she said, smiling at him.

"What does?" Ray asked.

"Saying what it is that you really want to say."

———————

There was steam rising up off the streets all around her as Emma made her way home. She knew with certainty that the humid air surrounding her had been pushing a hundred degrees before the rain came. She doubted the powerful but short storm had done much to lower the temperature either. What she couldn't understand was, in this sweltering heat, why was she still covered in goose bumps? Her dress and hair were barely damp anymore. There was no reason to be so chilled, but she was just the same.

Shivering, she wrapped her arms around her torso and fell into a light jog for the final few blocks.

She certainly hadn't admitted it to anyone, but Emma had come to associate the IGA with a boy her age who was carrying more of a weight on his shoulders than anyone ever should. She had made it a particular point to remember him and his family in her prayers all summer. It was hard to fathom what they were going through. The very thought was immensely unsettling to her.

She would find herself craning her neck every time she and her father drove by the store in his Plymouth. She'd try to peer past the glare of the windows to see if she could spot Ray at the cash register. When he was there, it seemed her heart would skip the tiniest of beats. She didn't know why it did that. She wondered if it had something to do with sympathy stimulating the blood flow.

A few times she had spotted him walking through the streets of East Prairie, most likely on his way home after a long and tiring day. She'd have to bite her lip to keep from calling out to him. Emma knew her parents would frown on her calling out to a boy she hardly knew. She wasn't a child anymore. Those days of freely calling out to boys were past her.

But it was her Christian duty to wish this boy well. The fact that her chest constricted every time she saw him, that had to be sympathy. The heat that burned on her cheeks when he had called out that strained good-bye—using her last name when she had no idea he actually knew it—well, to be honest, she didn't know *what* that was. All she knew was that when she blinked, she still saw his thick mass of dark, wavy hair—damp at the edges and swept back from his forehead—and his piercing hazel eyes that she would swear were saying more to her with each look than his lips ever did.

Emma sighed as she jogged up the steps of her front porch. It didn't matter if he was different from the other East Prairie boys or every bit the same. There was no real use finding out either. Emma had a plan for the next few years, and she had a plan all the years after that. She had a plan, and she wasn't going to deviate from it at all, not for anything, most certainly not for an East Prairie boy with dark skin, strong shoulders, and piercing eyes. Not for anything.

14

Worse than a Burr

The frustrating thing about humidity was that curls just wouldn't cooperate with it. Emma sighed as she stared at her reflection on the first day of school. No matter what she did, it felt as if her long black locks were sticking out in all the wrong places.

"Emma Givens," she whispered as she stared at her reflection. Her name sounded foreign and peculiar on her lips, the same way it sounded wrong when she sang out the songs she heard on the radio. She could sing them all she wanted, and her pitch was just fine. Everyone in church said so. But those songs still didn't sound right on her lips. She could sing them all she wanted, but they belonged to the singers who created them.

That was how her name felt rolling off her lips. Like the name Emma Givens should be spoken in a tight and tense baritone, a baritone that belonged to a boy her age who had lost his father and, God-forbid, if rumors held true, also a little brother.

A wave of frustration swept over her. Emma placed a damp palm over the bathroom mirror, smudging it immediately. "Emma Givens," she repeated aloud. She said her name over and over, each time more forcefully until she felt as if she owned the right to say it again.

Billie appeared in the doorway, studying her skeptically. "That's your name, don't wear it out."

Emma rolled her eyes. "Don't I know that?"

"Then why are you saying it?"

"Because I am, that's why. Are you ready, Billie? We need to get walking."

It was Billie's first day of high school, and she had been in a tizzy all week. Emma's father was already gone, but she trudged through the multitude of kisses and well-wishes of her mother, who asserted that two prettier girls had never been born.

The walk to school wasn't far. Emma could feel Billie's general nervousness as they entered the schoolyard. It was a rush of noise and bodies and commotion.

Beside her, Billie took a deep breath and smoothed out the front of her dress.

"Do you remember how to get to your first class?" Emma asked.

Billie nodded.

"Then I'll see you after school. Don't worry, Billie. Everything will be just fine."

As soon as Emma stepped into the hallway, she felt relieved. How could she ever be nervous in a school building?

For the most part, her classes were just a continuation of the year before: English, history, French, geometry, and cooking. By the time she sank down into the seat of her third-hour geometry class next to Loranna, Emma felt fully back into the swing of things. Then, to her surprise, Ray Rowe filed into the room and sank down into the empty seat at her right. This set her insides into a flutter all over again. He nodded her way then stared down at his desk, fumbling with the notebook in his hand.

Steeling herself, Emma turned toward him. "Looks like I was right. We have at least one class together. Ray, I'd like you to meet my friend Loranna. Loranna, this is Ray Rowe. He just moved to East Prairie with his family this summer."

Loranna's eyebrows shot up into her forehead at the sound of Ray's name. Of course she had heard about him. At this point, everyone in East Prairie had.

"Welcome to East Prairie, Ray."

Ray nodded affably at Loranna then looked back at his notebook. Suddenly embarrassed, Emma looked away. He might have an olive complexion, but she was fairly certain he was blushing too.

He didn't try to speak or even look her way again. Emma did her best not to notice him, but it felt like he was burning into her field of vision all the same. Even though he never volunteered the answer, Emma noticed how he came up with the correct answer to every question Mr. Donnelly asked and jotted it down in his notebook. Ray seemed to have no inclination to share his advanced math skills with anyone else though. He kept all these answers to himself, even when several hands popped up and their owners announced a string of wrong ones.

When the bell finally rang and class was over, Emma found herself searching for something else to say to him. There had been so many empty seats, and he had come in and sat right beside her. It had to mean something.

"Those boys I was talking about to you earlier, if you'd like I could meet you out front after school and introduce you to a few," she said, her heart hammering in her chest.

Ray's mouth dropped open an inch as he stood up from his chair and rested his notebook and new book against his hip.

"Thanks, Emma," he said, "but I can't stay after today. I'm needed at the IGA as soon as class is out."

"Oh."

"Thanks though." It wasn't his clipped words but the intensity in his gaze as he looked at her that made Emma's palms sweat in anticipation.

Emma glanced at the chalkboard for no reason at all and reminded herself that she didn't care about boys. From behind her, she could feel Loranna's warm breath on her neck. Emma was certain Loranna was soaking in every ounce of this awkward moment.

"I...I like your dress Emma," Ray finally said into the lingering silence between them.

There was a short burst of stifled giggles as the last of the kids exited the room, gawking at the three of them as they went.

For a brief moment, Emma found herself wondering if she could faint from embarrassment. "Thanks," she managed.

Loranna grabbed her arm and pulled her into the hall, and then she burst into hysterics. Emma frowned and poked her friend in the back.

"He'll hear you," Emma warned, following Loranna down the hall.

"You never said he liked you, Emma." Loranna shook off the laughter and held her hand loosely over her chest. "Oh boy, oh boy."

"That's because that would be a silly thing to say. We hardly know one another."

Loranna laughed again and craned her neck in the direction that Ray had disappeared. "Oh, Emma, at the sad way your conversation was flowing, it's going to take you two an eternity to get to know one another."

By the end of the first week of school, Emma was beginning to wonder if Loranna was right. Ray had two classes with her, geometry and English. In geometry, he had claimed the seat right beside her. In English, he sat directly behind her; the seats to her sides had already been taken when he walked in.

He had lunged for her pencil once when it had fallen. And then in English, when she was passing back a stack of papers, their fingers had brushed, and Emma had jerked the same as if she had been shocked.

To Emma's dismay, their conversations had grown more awkward rather than less. At least once a day, they would each falter to find something to say to the other, but each time it felt further than ever before to Emma from the natural conversations she had with the rest of her friends.

He was smart for certain, not only in math but in English too. Emma had only to pass back the first pop quiz in English to see his shining hundred percent to know that. Most of the other boys nearby had been grumbling about

Cs, Ds, and Fs. Emma had glanced back to find his cheeks red. She suspected he was thankful not to have been called out on his phenomenal grade.

He was a smart boy, but he didn't necessarily want everybody knowing it. She suspected he got enough attention being the boy supporting his family at the young age of fifteen. For being the boy whose father had suffered such a horrific death. For being the boy who lived on the wrong side of the tracks and spent just about every ounce of free time working at the IGA or taking care of his family.

As the first week of school slipped by into the second, and the second into the third, and then the first month into the second, their conversations grew no less awkward. However, Emma still couldn't escape the feeling that they were somehow together, a couple even.

Whenever she looked his way in the halls, his eyes were already on her. When they sat close in class, he almost never met her gaze, but he was still tirelessly attentive. If she dropped a pencil or needed a sheet of paper, she found him placing the item on her desk before she even knew what was happening. One afternoon, she slipped in the cafeteria and dropped her tray. He was beside her in a second, helping her with the mess even though his doing so sent the students in the cafeteria into an uproar of laughter and exaggerated smooches. He held the door for her whenever there was an opportunity and pushed in her chairs even before she could do so herself.

It was a dark and cloudy November afternoon when Emma finally felt she could take the suspense no longer. She wanted some sort of answer for his peculiar behavior, and she was determined to get it. When he was held back at the end of the day to talk with his last hour teacher, Emma saw an opportunity for a moment alone and seized it. Rather than walking out of the building with Loranna and Billie as was her habit, she urged them on without her and hung by her locker. She hoped he would come across her alone in the hall and be more prone to talk to her than when the classes and halls were crowded with other kids.

With nothing truly to do at her locker as the halls emptied of students, Emma riffled through her books and attempted to appear as if she was concentrating hard on something. Soon enough she noticed, out of the corner of her eye, a person walking down the hall toward her. The figure came to a standstill a few feet away.

"Hello, Emma."

Even having suspected that it was him approaching, Emma felt herself jump. Her cheeks felt warm as she turned to face him. "Hello, Ray."

A silence fell between them, and Ray rocked back on his heels. "Are you staying after today?"

"No." Emma shook her head, sending her loose curls tumbling over her shoulders. "I was just...I needed something, but I'm getting ready to leave now."

Ray swallowed. "I could walk with you."

"That would be nice," Emma replied, faltering for something else to say. She turned back toward her locker, grabbed an extra notebook, and slammed it shut.

He fell into step beside her in silence. It wasn't until they were headed down the brick steps out front that either of them spoke next.

"I'll carry your books," Ray offered.

Emma held them out skeptically. She was fairly certain the walk would be easier if she had a way to keep her hands busy.

"Do you have to work at the IGA today?" she asked, pulling at the first thought that came to her.

"Yeah, same as ever. Except Wednesdays. I get Wednesdays off."

"I didn't know that. How...how's your family, Ray? Your mother, is she okay?"

"My mother's okay. She keeps too busy *not* to be okay."

"Like you then, huh?" Emma offered him a feeble smile. "You are okay too, aren't you?"

Ray glanced over at her as they fell into step beside one another on the sidewalk in front of the school.

"I'm okay. I just...try not to think about it mostly."

Emma shuddered. "I couldn't imagine not having my father around."

"I've heard Mr. Yans, my boss, talk about him. He says your father is as good a man as there ever was."

"It's true," Emma said even though the words made her blush. "It sounds like I'm bragging, but I don't mean it that way. My father is just a wonderful person. So is my mother."

"I would have figured as such."

"How come?"

Ray shrugged but offered nothing in response.

"My little brother and your little brothers, I think they're friends at school. They play together on the playground."

"Are they? Art and Don hardly sit still long enough at home to talk much about school. When they do sit still, they tend to fall asleep mighty quick."

Emma laughed. "I've seen them once. I'm not surprised." Emma felt a wet drop on her arm and glanced up at the dark clouds. As she did, another large drop landed on her forehead. "It's been looking like it was going to rain," she added.

Ray glanced up at the sky but said nothing.

"Do you like it here, Ray?"

"Here as in East Prairie or here as in school?" he asked, motioning back toward the building that was still visible behind them.

"Both, I guess."

"I like it just fine. No one else here knows this, but my whole life before now, I lived in a big canvas tent. It was just one room, a wood floor, and all of us. It was simple back then. We were ruled by the river, whether it was too low or too high and getting ready to slide over its banks. Here, most no one thinks much about the river, aside from the sharecroppers and the farmers. But even with them, it's different."

Emma opened her mouth to ask if he liked this life better or worse, but then shut it. One life of Ray's was without his father. The other was with him. It wasn't a very kind question.

The sporadic drops fell harder, spraying them with cold pellets. Ray shifted his armful of books and raised the side of his jacket over Emma's head in protection.

"Will you go back? To work on the river one day yourself?" Emma asked, hugging her arms to her chest. Her thin sweater felt like nothing in the cold fall breeze. With his jacket half over her and being so close to him, she could smell the lingering scent of his Bay Rum cologne drifting over her nostrils.

A half snort escaped at her question, and Ray shook his head adamantly. "No, I'll never work on the river."

Surprised by the strength of his response, Emma pursued the subject no further. "My house is just down here." Emma pointed to the street behind the elementary school. Ray fell into step automatically next to her as she turned. As if he knew the way to her house as well as she did.

Emma was at a loss as silence stepped in between them once again. Tired of searching for words that nearly all felt wrong, Emma's brows furrowed together without her knowing it.

"Emma, if you ever need anything..." Ray said when they neared her house.

He paused automatically on the street in front of it, lowering his coat as he passed her share of books.

"Like what sort of thing?" Emma asked. Somehow this was worse. The more certain she became that he liked her, the less certain she felt about anything.

"Well, just anything," Ray said with a certain finality. The raindrops were falling harder, so he nodded and stepped back from her. "I'll be late for work if I don't hurry. And you'd best get inside before you get soaked."

Emma frowned and resisted the urge to thwack him on the head with her books. "As a matter of fact, I need things all the time. All girls do."

It was there on the tip of her tongue suddenly, the urge to scream. Ray studied her, clearly shocked. He chewed on his lower lip as if wondering what he had done to make her so upset all of a sudden.

"What sort of things do you need, Emma?" His voice was soft.

"All sorts. Like for instance, just yesterday, Loranna mentioned one of Bobby's friends is fixing on asking me to the Christmas dance. I need to know what to say to him when he does."

Color rushed to Ray's tan cheeks. "What...What is it that you want to say to him?"

Emma groaned, suddenly furious without truly understanding why. She turned on her heel without giving him an opportunity to say anything else. She reached her front door in a matter of seconds. Just before slamming it behind her, she caught sight of Ray at the edge of her yard standing stock still, his mouth slightly agape as he stared after her.

"What is it, dear?" Emma's mother asked as the sound of the slamming door reverberated around the house. Magdalene stepped out from the kitchen, spotted the look on Emma's face, and frowned.

"Nothing, Mama." Emma struggled to pull her anger back in and slip a lid on it even though she really wanted to release it into the world.

"That doesn't look like nothing," Magdalene said, stepping forward and pressing a kiss onto her daughter's cheek.

"It's just that, well, the world would be a less confusing place if it wasn't half full of boys." Something sparked in her memory at these words, making the hair on the back of her neck stand on end. When she couldn't place it, she dismissed it.

Magdalene laughed and turned back toward the kitchen. "Maybe so, Emma, but you're old enough to know that two halves make a whole."

Before plopping down on her couch in the living room, Emma had to force her gaze away from the window and Ray as he walked briskly back down her street, headed for the IGA.

"Ray Rowe, you're worse than a burr, if I do say so myself."

15

In the Stairwell Again

Emma was standing at her locker the next morning when she heard a throat clear behind her. She started then turned to find herself looking into the now-familiar hazel eyes of Ray Rowe.

"Good morning, Emma."

"Hello, Ray."

"You look nice today."

"Thanks." From two lockers down, Emma heard a stifled giggle from one of the girls in her first-hour class. Ignoring it, Emma shoved down the now-familiar frustration she felt whenever Ray paid attention to her, saying so much with his eyes and so little with his lips.

He cleared his throat and shifted his weight to his right foot. "I'm sorry about yesterday."

"What are you sorry for exactly?"

Ray swallowed hard and shook his head as if to dismiss the giggles of the girl just off to his side. "That I didn't ask you to the Christmas dance. I was wondering if you'd like to go with me."

Emma pressed her eyes shut the briefest of moments. After falling to sleep every night for the last few months wondering exactly what Ray Rowe's intentions were, he was finally asking her to a dance. The fact that he had needed a little prompting didn't faze her.

Even though she tried to curtail it, a smile pulled at her lips as she answered. "Why yes, I would like to go with you to the Christmas dance, Ray. Thank you very much for asking me."

Ray glanced down at his feet, his cheeks were positively crimson.

"Ray?"

"Yeah?" he asked, having gathered the nerve to meet her gaze again.

Emboldened by his equal insecurity, Emma leaned forward. "Was that so bad?" she whispered.

Ray's eyes opened wide a split second, and his hand closed around her elbow. "No, it wasn't." There was a smile on his face when he turned away and headed down the busy hall toward his class.

Emma exhaled deeply and realized for the first time that she had been guarding her breath. She closed her locker and fell against it. She suddenly felt exactly like she did a few years prior on Christmas morning when she had longed for a porcelain doll for months but had felt it was beyond her reach. It had been a strange emotion that had nearly overwhelmed her when she woke up and realized that the doll was hers after all. She had found herself wondering if she really deserved something so special. Now that the obstacle of acquiring it was out of her way, had she actually earned the right to have it?

As Ray disappeared into the crowded hallways of her school, Emma found herself wondering the same basic things about him. Did she deserve this quiet, hardworking boy? This pillar of such a big and precarious family. And, if he truly was hers, how might it change those things in her life that she didn't want to change?

Emma's hand went into a fist involuntarily. She determined right then and there that whatever grew between them, she wouldn't allow Ray to alter her plans in any way. She had been determined to live her life a particular way for so long, the thought of living it any other way felt foreign and unnatural. Nor would she ever come between him and the busy and quiet life he led with his family. The life they counted on him to lead.

It would just have to be like that. She could see no other way.

⸺⚹⸺

Six weeks later, Judy Garland's voice singing "Over the Rainbow" was booming over the speakers of the gymnasium. Emma resisted the urge to hum along with it. She didn't want anything marring her memory of this moment, this remarkable moment that she hoped to bottle up and remember forever. "Over the Rainbow" belonged to Judy Garland. All the other girls in the world could hum along and secretly hope they could sing it just as well, but the plain truth was no one could sing it like Judy Garland.

Now, with girls singing and humming the song all around them, Emma danced in Ray's arms, drinking in his now-familiar scent. Her thoughts became temporarily fixated on his scent. She wondered if, after it passed her nostrils and she pulled it into her lungs, did it travel around her body and get stuck in strange places? She wondered if she breathed in his scent long enough, would little parts of him become parts of her?

She smiled at the thought even though she knew it was silly. She rested her head on his shoulder as they moved around the dance floor. It became a game of memorizing the feel of his body next to hers. Wearing heels as she was, Ray was hardly any taller than her. Ray's body, however, was strong and solid and muscular where hers was soft and yielding. Emma and Ray. Ray and Emma. They matched up perfectly, practically melting into one another.

Emma found herself wishing she could feel what he felt, think what he thought. She wanted to truly understand him once and for all. She wanted to stop pulling at his sparse words and soaking in all the rest that he gave her in his gaze and in the feel of his hand when it pressed against her arm or her back. She wanted to *know*.

"Can I get you anything, Emma?" he asked quietly when the song ended and they pulled apart but kept standing in place.

"What do you think about when we're dancing?" she asked, refusing to step back from him, back from the windows that were his eyes.

Ray shrugged and glanced away, shutting her out of his thoughts. "Mostly I just think about not stepping on your feet."

"Are you happy here?"

Are *you* happy?" Ray asked, looking directly at her, suddenly and clearly alarmed.

"Yes, but I want to know you, and you won't tell me anything."

Ray's coloring looked almost green in the dim lights. Emma knew she was making him uncomfortable, but she pressed on. Kids she had known forever glanced their way, some snickering, others simply curious about the couple that stood on the dance floor unmoving.

"What is it you want to know?"

"Everything," Emma replied with an easy certainty.

"Everything is an awful lot," Ray protested.

"I don't care if it takes a while."

A soft smile spread across Ray's face, and he shook his head like he was part of some secret joke.

"Then I'll tell you, Emma, if you really want to know. Right from the beginning. My childhood is mostly a blur. I'm guessing that's because it was filled with so much of the same. But there's one part that's different from the rest, and I remember it very clearly. If you really want to know everything, I reckon I should start there."

Ray slipped her hand into his and pulled her across the dance floor. Bodies parted, still eyeing them curiously as they passed. Emma and Ray. Ray and Emma.

Emma bit her lip and forced back a rush of foreboding. It was as if she felt a whisper in her ear that nothing was ever, ever going to be the same again.

"What do you remember of the great flood, Emma?"

Emma shrugged. She assumed they were standing in a stairwell for privacy. It led to the second floor and was closed off from the rest of the building, trapping sound and air and adding to Emma's sudden unrest.

"I was a kid. We lost my house. We lost everything. I remember being afraid, and I remember it being dark. I remember being very sad about my dolls. Why do you want to know?"

"What else do you remember?" Ray asked, brushing the tips of his fingers over her cheek. "I brought you in here for a reason. Look around and tell me what else you remember."

Emma glanced around, confused. In the dim light, it suddenly felt as if the world was closing in on her. And she couldn't fathom why. Overwhelmed, she focused on Ray's lips. They were like beacons on a dark sea.

"I don't know what you mean. I was just a kid. I hardly remember anything from back then. Besides, there's nothing worth remembering anyway."

"I remember it," Ray said, letting his fingers trail down along her jawline, then down to her neck. "I remember feeling closed in because I had never been around so many people before. I remember needing to get away and finding a stairwell just like this. It was empty, and I played in it for hours."

Emma inhaled sharply. The world was closing in on her fast. Little flashes of memory tugged at her. A dress that wasn't hers, legs antsy from lack of movement, and a boy watching her from above in a stairwell.

"You were in East Prairie for the flood?" she implored. It wasn't true. It wasn't possible.

"Yes, my father was working on the river less than an hour away at the time. We and a dozen others were brought into town. We lived in the elementary school for nearly a month waiting for the flood waters to go down."

"Then we might have met back when we were kids?" Emma's voice faltered at the possibility.

"No, not *might* have. Tell me again what you remember. If you can't pull it back on your own, then I'll help you. But I want you to try first. Just try to remember."

"We must have played together," Emma said, shaking her head in frustration. It wasn't true. It wasn't possible. "I remember playing with lots of different kids."

"No." Ray dropped his hand and stepped back from her. "I brought you in here tonight for a reason. Tell me what you remember."

Emma swallowed hard as memories pressed in on her. Suddenly she could picture the boy's face from the stairwell all those years ago. Like a hard wind before a storm, it rushed in on her. "You are that boy on the stairs, aren't you, Ray? You have the same hair, the same eyes."

"Yes," Ray answered, obviously pleased. He slipped his hand into hers. "That was me. I had been sitting alone for hours then you came in and started hopping up and down the steps like a rabbit."

"I…I followed you up onto the roof. I haven't thought about that in years."

"Do you remember what happened up there?" His eyes were soft, kind, amused.

"We…We didn't kiss, did we?"

Ray laughed. "No, Emma, I was hardly in a space to be that bold. I was the coward, and you, you were the knight."

Emma's hand clapped over her mouth. "The door to the stairs! It was locked, wasn't it?"

"It was." Ray laughed and shook his head. "I was too terrified of heights to move. For years, I thought that if I could live that day over, I would be the one to lead us down that fire escape. I would do everything right and sweep you off your feet. But now I know. It had to be you. It *had* to be you, Emma. You saved me then. And now, when I need you the most, you're here to do the impossible all over again.

"You see, my brother died, Emma. In a terrible way. A way that sometimes you can't stand back up from. Everyone said I couldn't have done anything different. They said that even if I had, nothing would've changed. They said it was just Cecil's time to go. But none of that changes the fact that I should've found a way to do more for him that day. I should've kept him safe. It about killed me, losing him. Then, just when I thought I'd survive, we'd survive, there went my dad. In just as horrible of a death too. All of a sudden, I was stuck up on a roof again with all the doors locked and no foreseeable way down. And here you are once more, saving me when you don't even know you're doing it."

"Oh, Ray." Emma fell into his arms, her body shaking, and wrapped him in a tight embrace. "It's going to be okay," she whispered over and over. "It's going to be better now."

"I know it is, Emma." There was confidence in Ray's tone as he wrapped his arms around her in return. "I knew it was right from the very first time I saw you again. I was pretty much done believing in God—believing in anything. But then there you were, standing in my store, swearing under your breath about boys and how they made no sense. Right then and there, I knew that you were the answer to everything. It was like all the dots of my sad and crazy life connected finally and there was purpose and meaning to it. It's been easier getting by every day since."

Emma pulled back and shook her head, wiping off the warm tears that rushed down her cheeks. She shook her head abruptly and tousled her curls as a short laugh escaped her. "Oh, Ray, you don't fit into any of my plans, do you know that? Not a one. But here you are filling up the very center of each one anyway. How do you explain that?"

Ray grinned sheepishly. "My pa used to say some of the best things in life defied explanation."

When he leaned forward and brushed his lips against hers, Emma knew with a great certainty that nothing would ever be the same again. And for the first time in her life, she didn't care one bit.

16

War, Graduation, and Marriage

By the spring of 1941, it felt to Emma as if the world were one big teeter-totter. Sometimes it felt safe and wonderful and full of promise. In those moments, she wanted to hug herself and smile and hum the afternoon away. Other times it felt as if America were hovering on the brink of indescribable danger. The Great Depression was all but over, and its precarious economy was finally turning around as a result of increased industry. Europe was at war, and war was needy. This was generating a boom in America. However, the reports of invasion after invasion every night on the radio, of failed treaties and false hopes, and of democracies teetering on the brink of existence were terrifying to Emma.

It was a selfish thought, but she prayed every night that the war would stay bound up in Europe and not make its way into America. Hitler's regime had paraded into so many countries it hardly seemed believable. Then, too, tensions were rising in Japan. It was utterly terrifying, thinking how messy the war could become if tensions didn't cool down.

Sometimes, at night, she would awake with a start, having dreamt that Ray and her father had gone off to war. Once she even dreamt of little Richard with his still boyish fingers loading bullets into a rifle. Most often in her dreams, she would find herself searching for Ray. She moved through crowds of unknown people tirelessly, knowing that when she found him, she would be able to bring him safely home.

Her life was different now that she was sharing it with Ray. The fire of her passion was still burning in her chest, but now that passion was blanketed by the love, comfort, and the familiarity that being with him gave her. They would be together forever. Emma knew this with certainty even before he proposed to her midway through their senior year. They fit together like pieces of an interlocking puzzle, and life all around them became all the better for it.

Ray was happier and more content. He smiled and relaxed and even began to make friends with other boys his age. He doted on her almost to a fault, and Emma swore to herself that she would never allow herself to take advantage of it.

As the months passed by, Ray was starting to shine in all areas of his life. Even though he credited it to her, Emma knew it was only because he was finally allowing his potential to show through. At the IGA, Paul Yans had discovered Ray's talent with math. He had a natural way with numbers that gave him an understanding far greater than anyone else in Paul's employ. As a result, Ray had taken to overseeing the books when business was slow. He was bright enough to straighten out a terrible mess of numbers that Paul had never been able to sort out himself. Prior to

Ray's involvement, Paul hardly knew more than that there was enough money in the accounts when he had need of it.

When Emma told Ray he was smart enough to be anything he wanted, he dismissed her sheepishly and insisted that he already had everything he could ask for. By that, Emma knew that he mostly just meant her. Ray loved her. So much so that once in a while, Emma would feel a rush of disbelief at the thought. It was hard to comprehend that she could deserve such unbridled love and adoration as what Ray felt for her.

A full month before school let out and she was due to graduate, Emma's world seemed to be falling perfectly into place. She held her breath and hoped the war wouldn't step up to ruin it.

She had gotten word of a teaching position that would be open for the coming year in the farmlands on the outskirts of East Prairie. It was a small little nothing of an area not far from town, so small that the school house was only one room. It would be her job to teach all the sharecroppers' kids who attended, regardless of their grade or their acquired knowledge. She'd have to develop a system for teaching kids at varied levels. Once she began, she'd have a teaching job to call her own. It gave her the shivers thinking about it. She had dreamt about being a teacher ever since she could remember. Now it was rushing her way. She looked forward to it with nervous anticipation. She'd teach most of the year, breaking only for the long, hot summers and for cotton-picking in October. With Ray at her side, she'd have everything she ever wanted and more.

To add to Emma's delight, she and Ray were to be married as soon as their senior year was over and they had earned their diplomas. Before Ray came into her world,

Emma couldn't have conceived that lovesick feel that pulled at her stomach when he would come into view and offer her a private, sly grin. She also hadn't thought about marriage and sharing her life—all the peculiar moments of it—with another person. Now that she felt such love for Ray, it was as if she understood how the world was meant to work. Those silly fools over in Europe were causing such a raucous for nothing.

As the months and weeks ticked away, both graduation and her marriage drew closer. With luck, afterward, they'd rent a small house in town. Between the two of them working, they'd be able to forge a life of their own and still have enough to share with Mary, who would likely not be able to feed and care for all her children without Ray's support. Providing for his brothers and sisters was a burden that Ray had been forced to carry at a young age, but it was a necessary one, and neither he nor Emma would ever complain about the weight of it. Sometime soon, his siblings would grow up enough to provide for themselves. Until such time came, Ray could bear the burden without complaint. And so, too, could Emma.

━◦◦◦◦━

The morning of Emma and Ray's wedding dawned clear and bright. It was a perfect summer day, warm but with low humidity and the slightest of breezes to keep the heat from lingering too long in any one spot.

Magdalene, Billie, and Loranna fretted over Emma's hair and makeup in the small room in the basement of the Givens' church. Once, when the door that led to the hallway opened, Emma caught a glimpse of Ray passing by in a pressed Gabardine suit they had borrowed from a friend of her father's. They didn't make eye contact thankfully—Emma didn't want to risk any bad luck—but she felt her heart swell with pride at the sight of him. He was fit and handsome and well on his way to becoming as fine a man as her father.

Standing over Emma, still fretting over her appearance, Magdalene hooked a small blue flower pin on the slip just inside her dress.

"There you go, dear," Magdalene said, patting her shoulder. "We've covered all the bases now—old, new, borrowed, and blue. With the love you two have for one another, you don't need the luck, but it never hurts to be certain, does it?"

Emma smiled, slid the tube of lipstick over her lips a second time, and then pressed them together.

Behind her, her mother sighed and sank down into a nearby chair. "My baby, you'll never be our little Emma Givens again."

Emma stared at herself in the mirror and felt the truth in her mother's claim. What she couldn't find the words to explain was how the name Emma Givens hadn't belonged to her at all ever since Ray had called it out in good-bye that day of the storm, now nearly two years ago. He had claimed her name without meaning to, just as he had claimed the rest of her by loving her as much as he did.

Now she was to be Mrs. Ray Rowe or Mrs. Emma Rowe, depending on who was doing the talking. Emma Rowe was an entirely different sounding sort of person than Emma Givens. Emma figured that Mrs. Emma Rowe was seasoned and noble enough to lead any classroom, no matter how varied in age and education the students were. Mrs. Emma Rowe could also head up a household. She could see to it that hot and tasty dinners made their way to the table at a reasonable hour, and she could teach a whole passel of children along the way. Something about having the love of Ray made all those things not only possible but easily obtainable.

Behind her, Loranna finished pinning up Emma's hair, along with the fresh baby's breath that now framed her face, and stepped back to study her work.

"Emma, you are my best friend in the entire world, so I might be partial, but I do think you are the prettiest bride ever.

Emma smiled and squeezed her hand. "You'll be just as pretty on your wedding day, Loranna. And thanks to you, my hair looks wonderful."

Across the packed room, Billie stood in the corner, smoothing out the lower half of her dress. She turned to study her backside in the mirror.

"Billie, you look beautiful too."

"My legs though, Emma," she said, biting her lip.

Magdalene frowned as she studied her youngest daughter. "Billie, how many times do we have to tell you? Your legs are just as normal as every other girl's. And you're going to look just as beautiful up there as your big sister."

Billie blushed scarlet and chewed on her lower lip. "Thank you, Mama."

Magdalene sighed. "Loranna, will you take a picture of me with my two lovely daughters? After today, I'll only have one Givens girl left. Thank heavens for Richard. He'll carry on the Givens name at least." She stopped and shook her head. "Assuming he matures the way boys are supposed to, that is."

Emma laughed and drew tight against her mother. Her thoughts raced at her mother's words, and she tried to fight off a wave of anxiety. Tonight she would go to bed a wife. She and Ray would leave their childhood behind. Together, they would become woman and man, and for the rest of their lives, they would share a union with one another that would separate them from everyone else on this earth. It's what was truly meant by marriage in the first place, Emma realized. Two people would become one, and hopefully, they would become all the stronger for it.

When the knock on the door came ten minutes later, Emma's fears had somehow washed away. She didn't need to be afraid of becoming a woman or a wife or a teacher or even, one day, a mother. With Ray at her side, everything made sense, and there was nothing to fear.

She met up with her father, whose eyes immediately filled with tears at the sight of her, just outside the small room. Together, they followed the three women up the basement stairs of the church.

Ray was standing at the end of the aisle when the music started. His eyes were fixed on her in a way that made Emma feel like the only girl in the world. Emma straightened her shoulders and took a breath. Beside her, she could feel her father shaking as he led her down the aisle. There were tears in his eyes, spilling over and down his cheeks. Emma found herself wishing for a moment of privacy with him. She wanted to remind him that what she strove for was to hold Ray in a place of regard as high as she held him. She wanted to remind him that he wasn't losing a daughter. She had told him so a few times since Ray had asked his permission for her hand. She knew that he knew it down deep where it mattered, even if he was forgetting it during that long walk down the aisle while so many faces were watching.

Then suddenly, in a blur, it was just her and Ray and a set of quietly whispered vows, and the rest of the world fell away. When it was over and he kissed her, Emma laughed in delight. If only the whole world could know this feeling of perfection and belonging, there would never, ever be war.

17

The Most Important Thing

Gene Autry's "Jingle Jangle Jingle" was playing on the radio as Ray stood at the back door of the shabby duplex that he and Emma had rented for the last six months. It was mid-December of 1941, eight days after the bombings at Pearl Harbor and just four days after Hitler had officially declared war on America.

He stood on the threshold of the back door facing out into the darkened yard, feeling the heat from the furnace on his backside while the brisk December air stung his exposed face, neck, and hands. He smoked in the doorway because he knew Emma wasn't keen on the smell of it lingering in the house, even though she largely kept quiet about it.

He opened the palm of his left hand and caught a puffy snowflake. In less than a second, its perfect form dissolved into a speck of moisture, of nothingness. Snowflakes and their beautiful symmetry had fascinated Ray as a kid. Now, standing at his back door so late at night, unable to sleep over fear of the horror that was rushing their way, he found himself unexpectedly hating them. Hating how something so impossibly beautiful could also be so frail and insignificant. Hating how easy it was to wipe them out of existence. How they could simply cease to be—like the living, breathing beings that had been Cecil and his father—so permanent and alive one day, then nothing but a hollow shell the next.

He took a final drag on his cigarette, and then he smashed the butt into a nearby tray and closed the door. At the rate the flakes were falling, come morning it would be a winter wonderland outside.

Ray sighed and swallowed down a glass of water before heading to the bedroom where Emma was already fast asleep, exhausted from her long days of teaching and her evenings of cooking and tending to their home.

America was at war, and Europe was in one hell of a mess. Just like snowflakes, people were melting away into nothingness every moment. Whether it was under Hitler's direction or Japan's, it didn't matter.

He undressed and slipped under the sheets next to his new wife's soft, still form. It was a selfish thought that snaked across his mind. He wouldn't fight. No matter what was coming. He wouldn't risk making her a widow. If he had never met up with her again, things would be different. He'd probably have an itch to join up right away to defend his county. But somehow or another, she had become the single most important thing in his life, and even though he scarcely believed it, he understood that she doted on him nearly as much. He wouldn't risk it, leaving her alone. Not even to do a bit part in a justice that needed serving more than the world had ever seen. It was the one time in his life that he was going to allow himself to be selfish. Not for his sake, but for Emma's. That was how much she meant to him.

—⚬⚬⚬—

As the months passed, Ray began to prefer time in the stockrooms at the IGA or in office balancing the books far above any time he was forced to spend as a cashier. It was the talk of all the East Prairie townsfolk that was getting to him the most, making him feel like a snowflake on the verge of disintegrating. The information they carried to him was the same, although the names they discussed were different.

All everyone talked about was war. It seemed to be the mission of every man or woman too old to serve to remind Ray on a daily basis of another boy his age who had just enlisted. A boy who was doing his duty. A boy who was serving his country. A boy who intended to fight off the evil that was winding its way through the world.

With every new name he heard, Ray began to feel more and more distanced from himself. More and more distanced from reality. He reminded himself over and over that anything he could do to serve his country was likely to be less important than making sure Emma didn't become a young widow.

When she curled up into the sheets every night exhausted but pleased by her long days, he'd rub her calves before she fell to sleep. It became a game of trying to slip his hands down to rub her feet, an act which tickled her something fierce. She'd laugh and pull away and swear he was incorrigible.

They were two polar forces tugging at him at all times any longer—Emma and the war. For himself, he didn't fear death or pain or imprisonment. What woke him up in a cold sweat were his nightmares of Emma, old and alone and crying out for him in anguish.

He found himself praying to a god he wasn't certain he believed in that the war would end and the needless suffering over in Europe would stop. Then he wouldn't have to choose between the woman he loved more than anything in the world and making the decision that he felt in his gut was the right one.

Before he knew what was happening, the day came that changed everything.

<hr />

Emma was standing at the sink when Ray came home late from the IGA. There were raw pork chops in a pan on the counter and a small pile of potatoes in front of her, untouched. She was looking out the window and hardly noticed his arrival.

He shuffled over, lifted her hair, and kissed the back of her neck. It was early December, and America had been at war with Germany and Japan for two years.

Ray found himself surprised how quickly Christmas kept coming around anymore. Financially, they were scraping by. This was fortunate considering that nearly half of what they made they shared with Ray's family. There was even enough left over to buy a few presents for everyone. Deciding what to buy Emma every year troubled Ray something fierce. Before his return to East Prairie, he simply could not have fathomed ever wanting to please someone as much as he wanted to please her.

"Hey, darling," he said, pulling back from his kiss. "How was your day? Kids behave themselves?"

Startled out of her reverie, Emma set down the knife that had been dangling in her hand and turned to face him.

"Yes, as well as they ever do right before Christmas. Ray, there's something...there's something I need to tell you."

"Yeah? What is it?" He felt his insides turn cold in anticipation. Something had her out of sorts for certain.

She tossed her head, swept her hair from her face, and then took him by the elbow. "Let's sit, Ray. We never just sit and talk anymore."

"No," he replied, "we don't. Most especially not when you're smack-dab in the middle of dinner. What's going on, Emma?"

Emma sank down onto the sofa and patted the cushion beside her. "Please sit, Ray. I'm so nervous I can hardly think straight as it is."

Begrudgingly, Ray sank into the seat beside her.

"Did something happen at work?"

Emma shook her head. "It's more about what didn't happen. At least it didn't happen last month when it was supposed to happen, and it hasn't happened since. And now other things are happening too, like the fact that I can't stand to look at raw pork chops. And I was nauseous all day. At first I was so busy, I hardly thought about it. Now, I can't think about anything else."

"Emma, what are you saying?" Ray grabbed her hand in disbelief.

She bit her lip, curtailing a shy smile. "What I'm saying is I think we're going to have a baby."

Ray stared at her a moment in disbelief. Then he stood up and paced the small room, his heart hammering in his chest.

"It's not possible, Emma. Think about what you're saying."

Emma laughed and covered her mouth with one hand. "Not possible? Honestly Ray, think about what you're saying. It *is* possible. Come to think about it, I'm just surprised it's taken so long."

Ray stopped in his tracks and ran his fingers through his hair. "Emma, there's a war going on. It's not really the time for having babies, is it?"

Emma's smile faltered. "You're not happy then? I thought...I thought you wanted children."

Letting out a massive breath, Ray sank down onto the sofa and wrapped her in his arms. "Emma, there's nothing more I could want in the world than for you to have my baby. It's just...there's a war going on. The whole world is going crazy, and you're going to have a baby. How am I supposed to feel about that?"

Emma felt tears sting her eyes. It was true what he was saying. A little human had taken root in her belly, and now she was going to bring it into a world where all everyone talked about was war and death. A world where boys from school, boys she had known since childhood, went off to serve and never came home.

But it wasn't going to happen to them. "It's okay, Ray. You're right, the world is going crazy. But you aren't. You're sane and stable, and you're right here in East Prairie. You're safe. *We're* safe. God willing, the war will never make it this far."

A dry laugh escaped him. "The thing is, for a while now, I've been thinking that maybe holing up in the IGA of East Prairie, Missouri while able-bodied men all over the world are taking up a fight bigger than themselves ain't the right thing to do. Hell, this here war has become bigger than everybody. If Europe falls, Hitler will be setting his sights on America next. Everybody knows it."

"Then wait and stay here. Stay safe."

"I've wanted to enlist for a while now, Emma. The only reason I haven't is because I'm afraid of leaving you alone. But I've come to realize that you aren't alone. You have your parents, your brother and sister, and now you're going to have our baby."

In numb disbelief, Emma sat there staring at her husband of nearly two and a half years. There was a look of sorrow blended with determination in his eyes that she had never seen before. Right then she understood that no matter what she did, Ray had somehow or another already made the decision to enlist in a great and terrible war. She could lose him. The thought rushed through her like floodwater, seeping into every inch of her body.

She wrapped her arms across her chest and pulled away from him. "I think…I think I want to lie down."

"No, not yet." Ray shifted on the couch and closed his hands over Emma's shoulders. "Listen to me, Emma. You have to understand. You have to know why I need to do this. God knows I love you more than I ever should. If he's really up there anyway, letting all this insanity run loose and doing nothing to stop it. But regardless, I love you more than anyone should ever love someone. It puts me in your power in a way that you don't even know. I'd do anything for you if you asked, and I'd ask for nothing in return. But for my sake, I need to ask you something now."

Emma wiped away a tear as she studied him. It was true. He had never once asked her for anything. She felt her stomach lurch in fear. She wasn't sure if it was the baby inside her or fear that made her want to vomit. Either way, she knew she'd never be able to hold down dinner.

"What do you want to ask me, Ray?" she said, knowing very well that she'd have to say yes to whatever a husband who never asked for anything finally asked for.

"You're going to have my child. A boy or a girl, it doesn't matter. But when he—I'll say he for the sake of it—grows up and goes to school and listens to some lady like you teaching him about the war, and he comes home to ask what his daddy did to help, the answer can't be to hole up in the IGA, Emma."

"And it can't very well be get himself blown to pieces either, Ray," Emma said, sobbing.

Ray sighed and wrapped her in a tight embrace. "It won't be, I promise."

"You can't promise that." Emma sniffed and wiped her nose.

"I'll find my way home. That there's a promise. Just you wait and see. I'll find my way home."

Waiting and hoping became a feverish game in the Rowe household the next few months. Once Emma consented to Ray's enlistment, he promised to stay through the holidays. By New Year's Eve, Emma was nearly overpowered by morning sickness. Women all around swore it would wane soon. Unable to leave while she was out of sorts, Ray committed to staying home long enough for it to subside. All the while, Emma prayed the war would end before it did.

It didn't.

Near the end of February, Ray came home in an unusually quiet mood while Emma was making dinner. His cheeks were pale, and he didn't attempt to hold Emma's gaze when he pulled away from planting a kiss on her cheek.

"What is it?" Emma grabbed his hand to prevent him from turning away.

His body still half-turned, he reluctantly looked into her eyes.

"It was time, Emma. It was more than time. I enlisted today."

Feeling her knees grow weak, she dropped his hand and sank into a kitchen chair. "Even before you came home, I suspected as much."

"How is that?"

"The sun was out, and there was a warmth in the air that there hasn't been in months. Of course it would be the promise of spring—of renewal—that would remind you of your intentions of heading to a world of death and darkness."

"I didn't need to be reminded of it, Emma." Ray stood over her, brushing her silky hair back from her face with his fingertips. "I think about it every day. I think about how leaving you and that baby growing in your belly will be the hardest thing I figure I'll ever have to do. Maybe even harder than living with the shame the rest of my life if I don't."

"If I begged you to stay, would you do it?"

"You won't. That isn't who you are and it's part of why I love you so much."

"Then promise me, at any cost, that you'll live, Ray."

"You know that I will do my best, that's all—"

"No, that's *not* all." Emma paused for a second, choking back angry tears. Then, with an angry shake of her head, she continued. "There is no better or best when it comes to living. There's being alive, and there's not being alive. I need you to come home alive. That's all there is to it. I knew

Donnie Summerton my whole life, and he didn't survive five weeks in combat. But there are plenty of men who did. They managed to be in the right place at the right time. They dodge bullets and who knows what else. And they are coming home to their wives and mothers and children. I need you to be one of these men, Ray. God knows it's selfish, but I *need* you to be one of these men."

Feeling his heart rip in half from the determination on her face, Ray sank to his knees and pressed his forehead onto her thigh. He exhaled slowly and pressed the palm of his hand against her swollen, taut belly. He opened his mouth to make a promise that wasn't his to make. As he did, he saw himself kneeling by his wife, and he felt removed from his own life for the first time in his recollection.

It was a sin most likely, making a promise that wasn't humanly possible and knowing that, somehow, he'd have to keep it.

"Don't worry yourself, baby. Just you watch. I'm going to come home to you. That there's a promise."

———

A small crowd assembled at the train station the morning of Ray's departure. There were Ray's mother, Mary, his brothers and sisters, Emma, her parents, and the other two Givens children with a few friends as well. Taking it in, wishing he could commit every detail to memory, the thought occurred to Ray that they hadn't all been together since the day he and Emma were married. That was the way of things, he figured. Weddings and funerals and war brought people together in a way that everyday life didn't.

A thick, gray blanket of clouds covered the sky, and an endless drizzle splattered down from it. Tiny drops of water landed on his wife and family. The droplets were so small that they didn't sink into their clothes for some time. Instead, the tiny beads held together and glistened in the incandescent light spilling out from the station, helping to preserve the moment.

Dick Givens squeezed Ray's shoulder affectionately. "You come home safe, son. You hear?"

Ray nodded and said that he did.

There was something about worry that made people look older. Dick was a strong man and a healthy one at that. This was the first time Ray thought he had looked older than his years.

A dozen feet away, the twins were huddled together next to the idling train. A smile pulled at the corner of Ray's mouth when he watched them set a penny on a bit of exposed track.

Art met his gaze and shrugged. "It's for luck," he said.

Ray thought of the wedge of wood from the massive tree trunk that had killed his father that he had packed into his bags. Why he had brought it along he didn't know, but it had felt wrong to leave it behind.

"If it's for luck, then be sure to take care of it," Ray said.

"We will."

Good-byes were said in a quick rush of emotion. He felt numb and once again removed from himself when it came to saying good-bye to his wife, whose swollen belly pressed into his hip when she draped her arms around him.

"Take care of yourself. Take care of our baby."

Emma swallowed back a fresh bout of tears. "You know that I will. It's you that I'm—"

Ray pressed his thumb over her lips. "Don't."

Emma's eyes widened with understanding. She cupped his hand in hers and pressed it to her cheek. "It's going to be fine."

The drizzle switched to steady rain just before Ray boarded the train, causing him to rush the good-byes so his memory of all of those he held so dear wouldn't be of them soaked to the bone in the gray, wet morning.

The train lurched forward shortly after he was seated, its wheels screeching on metal. From his window, Ray waved to the group that belonged to him. Don and Art shoved one another as they fought for space under the packed awning. Ray thought of the penny placed on the tracks and wondered if the twins would remember it.

Emma placed one hand on her belly; with the other, she blew him a kiss. Her cheeks were wet from more than rain. Ray pressed his hand to the glass and left it there until they were no longer in sight. He settled back and closed his eyes.

One of the few things he remembered of his early childhood, aside from being stuck up on the roof with Emma, was an afternoon he spent one fine spring day playing on the banks of the river with some of the kids from camp. They had been running and laughing and chasing one another, and Ray had been perfectly happy. It was one of the few memories he had of complete and perfect happiness. Floods, tension, hunger, and death had snuck into so many others that he no longer felt such pure, unbridled emotion.

Emma made him happy, happier than he had ever been in his adult life. But it was a different sort of happiness than what he had experienced as a child. Happiness for him now was often clouded with the threat of impending loss, or the possibility of loss. Of knowing that he loved Emma so much that he couldn't stand to live without her. Of waking up in a cold sweat after dreaming that the Nazis were flying over East Prairie, dropping bombs on everything in sight.

He was headed out on a train, leaving behind everyone he loved. He was headed for grueling training and then into a gruesome war, but he was less afraid than he had been in a very long time.

Whatever happiness he and Emma were to have, he was going to do his part to ensure it. That's all he was capable of doing.

18

Bivouac

A piercing whistle followed by a chaotic shuffling came from the front of the night-darkened bunk. It was nearing the end of twelve weeks of training, and Ray was accustomed to being roused from the depths of sleep to fumbling into his uniform with clumsy fingers and a sluggish mind that wouldn't properly command them.

"Where to this time?" Martin grumbled beside him, although he knew quite well, of course, that they were somewhere close to the US Army training facility at Camp McCain, in a swampy forest, in the middle of Mississippi.

"I reckon we'll figure it out when we get there. Same as we always do," Ray answered.

"Yeah, well, a little communication never hurt anyone, now did it?" Martin replied.

Jimmy, from two cots down, fumbled for his boots in the darkness and shot a smart remark their way even though no one had addressed him. "You think them Nazis is gonna communicate with you when they send a bunch of grenades our way? Like you get to claim 'no fair, I wasn't ready' on them?"

"Shut your pie hole, Jimmy, or I'll shut it for ya." Martin arched his back, ready for a fight that wasn't coming his way.

Jimmy finished tying his boots and fumbled, with the rest of the infantry, out the bunk entrance. No man could be certain, but it was either too late in the evening or too early in the morning to pick a fight with a fellow sleep-deprived soldier.

Ray piled out too with the rest of the men into the darkness that awaited them. Sore, overworked muscles protested in his legs, arms, and back as he walked. He was tired of training and ready to head into war. Tired of drills and fear of what lay ahead, scared stiff by the idea of what might be coming. It wasn't so much that he had been naive with regard to the horrors of war before enlisting. It was that he had a greater respect for it now. Ray's individualized training had been on how to fire bazooka bombs. Nothing survived their blasts. Then, too, the regular bullets he shot daily pulverized their wooden targets, creating a splinter of shrapnel in their wake. Ray still felt humbled by the way wood disintegrated in the face of a bullet. He had a deeper respect now at the idea of them piercing his flesh. A deeper respect over the prospect of being burnt alive or losing his limbs in a grenade blast. A deeper respect for all the ways to die that war inflicted on men around the world.

Ray sighed and fell into step with the men of his infantry unit, most of whom he now considered to be intimate friends.

Nearly twelve weeks of training had accomplished that. Like his buddies surrounding him, he was bone-tired, and he found himself wishing for a way to sleep while walking. For the moment, the men's side talk was quiet. They were still too sluggish to find words of humor or complaint. All that could be heard were the barks of their commanding officers intent on yet another night drill, the stamping and uneven shuffling of dozens of feet making their way in the darkness, and the roar of a diesel motor in the distance.

It was nearing the end of May, and they were shipping out in two days. Rumors had been pouring through camp like wildfire. There was something big in the works. Everyone knew it, but almost no one could say with any certainty what it was. From what Ray could figure, they were headed to England and would join a large group of soldiers in an attack on occupied France. Where in France he wasn't sure, but if rumors held true, it was going to be the most ambitious invasion by Allied forces to date.

He hoped for a chance to talk to Emma before he shipped out, but he wasn't certain he was going to get it. The last he had talked to her, her belly was big and swollen, and she felt certain the baby would be coming any day now.

The thought of his wife and unborn child sent a crazy rippling of emotion through him again. Some primal need to make the world safe for them, greater than anything he had ever felt.

Beside him in the darkness, Martin tripped on a rock and slammed into him, nearly knocking Ray off balance.

Instinctively, Ray grabbed Martin by the elbow and didn't let go until they both had found solid footing. The roar of the crawler truck that had been approaching caused the long line of men to contract as they made way on the jagged trail through the forest for it to pass.

From a few feet behind them, Jimmy shot another snide remark their way. "What's with you, Martin? Do you need your buddy to do your walking for you?"

Having weathered one too many of Jimmy's retorts since the onset of training, Martin whipped around, ready for the fight he had been longing for.

Sensing a scuffle, there was an outburst of movement from all around. Bodies shifted as they walked to get a better view. Ray twisted around and felt his heel catch on the foot of the guy in front of him.

It happened so fast he had no time to feel fear or to react. As he fell directly into the path on the oncoming crawler truck a split second before it reached them, he had no time for anything. A single word left his lips as he slammed onto the ground and the massive tank-like tracks bulldozed relentlessly over him and his world went black.

"Shit."

———

Emma opened her eyes to the first light of day. As always, it took a second to familiarize herself with her surroundings and to the state of her body for reality to sink in. Most likely it was the sight of her old room greeting her every morning that caused her to wake up with a start. She was a married woman of twenty. She was a teacher, and she had a house of her own. Any day now, she would give birth to the baby that had taken up residence in her body, consuming more space than she would ever have thought possible.

With Ray headed off to war, the only natural answer had been for Emma to go home again. To wind back the years and live with her parents once more.

Rolling over in bed, Emma stretched carefully, remembering the pain that doing so sometimes sent rippling through her midsection. From the kitchen, Emma could hear the soft murmurings of her parents. She smiled to herself at the soft, easy, and comforting sound. When the war was over, she wondered if she and Ray could ever imagine being like her parents had always been to her.

Through the glass panes of her window, Emma could hear the tinkling sounds of laughter in the distance. East Prairie kids headed past the big, shaded playground on their way into school. She wondered if it was fate that the big elementary school had become such an intricate part of her life. She and her family had found shelter in it during the flood of the century just months after it was built. Although she could not have conceived it at the time, she had met the love of her life there. Months later, she was enrolled in school in it. Years later, her father had built the quaintest home in the world just behind the shade of the massive trees that protected the playground.

Her life would come full circle one day when she would be offered a teaching position there. She didn't know how she felt it with such certainty, but she did all the same. It wasn't that she didn't enjoy teaching in the rural one-room schoolhouse, a half-hour drive out from town. It was a challenge, teaching kids with such a large range in age. She moved about all day. She lined them up in rows according to their age and moved about throughout the day, giving lessons to one group and then to the next. It was tiring and a challenge, and she would do it forever if it wasn't for the fact that it was her calling to teach at the R. A. Doyle Elementary School that had been such an intricate part of her life since she was just a child.

Three weeks prior, Emma had stopped teaching and gone on maternity leave. She wished she had been able to finish the school year, but her body was protesting, and Dr. Whitaker had said it wasn't good for the baby to continue on her feet like she was doing every day. So she left her children in the care of an interim teacher and took up residence once again in her parents' house.

Their baby would be born in this house within earshot of the playground and school that had already defined so much of her life already. The only thing that would make it better was if Ray were here to experience it with her.

She no longer feared for his life. She couldn't explain it fully, the way she had given up the fear. He would miss the birth of his child, but he was coming home to her, safe and sound. She didn't know *how* she felt it with such certainty, but she did. After all, he had promised. And if she knew anything about Ray Rowe, it was that he was a man who kept his promises.

Once she had stretched enough that her body felt ready to bear the cumbersome weight of her taut, swollen belly, Emma tossed back her covers and cautiously stepped to her feet. She felt the muscles tense in her feet, legs, hips, and lower abdomen as she stood. Her thin, petite frame seemed to have shrunken in all other places aside from her belly as the baby grew inside her. Her stomach was so enormous now that there was hardly room for her to eat or catch her breath.

It was a struggle to sit on the toilet, but Emma relieved her overly full bladder before heading into the kitchen. She rolled her hands up and down the mountain of her middle body as she stepped into view of her parents who were sitting at the table. She waited for the pleased clicking of her mother's tongue as she took in sight her daughter's swollen belly and the daily exclamation that she would never have been able to carry such a large baby so well.

It wasn't coming though. Emma knew it as soon as she saw her mother's puffy, red eyelids. Emma's breath caught in her throat.

"Mama, what on earth is wrong?" Emma asked as she beelined to her mother. Her father had been sitting at the table with his back to her. As Emma made it to her mother's side, she was shocked to find that her father's lids were just as red and swollen.

"Dear God, Mama, is it Billie?" Emma's sister had married young and had been causing all sorts of mischief lately.

"Sit, baby," Magdalene said, patting the chair beside her.

Emma surrendered and sank into it more from the fact that her knees gave way at the horror of the unknown than as an effort to obey her mother. Beside her, Magdalene's shoulders shook as she covered her face in one hand and closed the other over Emma's knee.

Emma felt the fear rising into her throat, taking up all the rest of the space that the baby didn't. "Daddy, I can't stand it. What is going on?"

Dick swiped at his eyes with one hand and reached across the table to cover her hands with his other one. "I'm afraid it's too early to tell you anything with any certainty, Emma, and the day promises to be a long one. For it's unlikely we'll know anything with any certainty for several hours."

"You're not making any sense. What is it? Tell me, Daddy. I can't take seeing Mama like this."

"Emma, baby, it seems…it seems Ray was injured last night. We don't know his condition. We won't for several hours."

Emma shook her head in disbelief. "That's not possible. He hasn't even gone off to war. He's just in training still. You can't get hurt in training. It has to be a mistake, Daddy. They have the wrong man. They have to."

Dick shook his head and brushed away a fresh tear. "It was a night drill, baby. An accident, that's all."

"Someone shot him? By accident?" Emma felt as if she were swimming—drowning even—in a sea of disbelief. "I don't believe it."

Emma felt her mother's arms wrap around her shoulders while her sobs shook her body.

"He wasn't shot, baby," Dick continued. "He was run over."

Emma went numb, and her ears began to ring. "Run over. No, it's not possible. How do you know this? Did you hear his voice?"

"No, Emma. I spoke with the sergeant."

She shook her head involuntarily. "They have the wrong man. They have to."

"It's unlikely the army would make that sort of mistake. All we need to focus on now is that he was alive when they put him on the train. The sergeant said he was hanging on—just—but they couldn't do much of anything for him in camp aside from stabilizing him for the journey. They set his leg and put him on a train for Tennessee. There's a veteran's hospital there that has some of the best doctors in the world. If he survives the trip, he'll be in good hands."

"*If…*" Emma pushed away from her mother and stood up, wrapping her hands protectively around her belly. "Then we're going to Memphis too."

Dick rose to his feet and placed his large, weathered hands on top of Emma's shoulders from across the small table. "Sit yourself back down, Emma. You've got his child to protect, and you aren't in a state to be standing right this minute, much less getting on a train. You know as well as we do that Dr. Whitaker wouldn't allow you to even travel to the train station today, much less board a train. Ray's job is to hang on until he gets to Memphis, where they can get him some help. Yours is to stay put and deliver that baby when the time comes. There's no more to it."

Emma felt herself sinking back into the chair against her will. Her body was so numb it wouldn't hold her, whether or not she willed it to. Her mother wrapped her in a hug once more. It felt to Emma like she was miles away and not really touching her.

"Tell me everything they told you, Daddy. Just as they told you. Don't keep anything from me because you think I can't handle it. It's the not knowing that will kill me worse than the knowing."

Dick let out a long, slow exhale and sank back down into his seat across from her. "I believe you, Emma. I'll tell you everything they told me, but it wasn't much. It was a crawler truck. The damn new one they've been advertising lately."

Emma's eyes shot wide in alarm as she pictured the truck's massive track wheels—half tank, half truck.

"He slipped and fell in the mud. It ran full over him before the driver even knew he had fallen."

"Where did it hurt him?" Emma's voice sounded hollow and far away. Like someone else's.

"They say one leg's mashed up pretty bad. They set it the best they could before putting him on the train. He got it in the chest too. One lung is fully collapsed and the other one nearly so. He was unconscious when they called but still had a faint pulse. The work they did on his leg knocked him out, which is probably for the best. They put him on the first train to Memphis. If he's alive when they arrive, his odds of survival will improve. The sergeant..." Dick took a deep breath and swallowed before he was ready to continue. "He said that we should prepare ourselves for the worst. He said, truth be told, he shouldn't be alive at all. He said that kind of weight would take the life clear out of anyone, and there isn't much reason to hope."

Emma's vision sharpened as she looked at her father. "Well, he's wrong, Daddy. And he doesn't know Ray. Ray's going to live, and he's going to come home. He promised me he would, and Ray Rowe keeps his promises. He always does."

Dick nodded, and his shoulders shook at the look of determination on his daughter's face. "You're right at that, Emma. Ray is a man to keep his promises. If it's humanly possible, I reckon he'll find a way to hang on until they can get him some help. That's all we should think on today. That and the safety of that baby of his you're about to bring into this world."

<hr />

In the Kennedy Veteran's Hospital, just before lunch on May 25, 1944, a train arrived carrying a member of the US Army Corps of Engineers who was pathetically near death. Considering the fact that America was in the midst of a terrible war, the arrival of such a passenger shouldn't have been such an extraordinary occurrence. However, by the time they were shipped in from overseas, most of the men treated in Memphis's veteran hospital were not in immediate danger of death.

But this soldier had not been to war; he was not arriving from Europe, and his wounds were in no means typical. He was, in fact, the first soldier to have been run over by one of the five-ton crawlers and still have a breath of life left in him, no matter how pathetic that breath seemed.

His arrival in the surgical suite of Kennedy rose more than a few eyebrows of the surgeons on duty. With a crushed rib cage, partially collapsed lungs, likely internal bleeding, and a pulverized hip and leg, he was little more than a corpse. But he was hanging on and floating in and out of consciousness. He had survived a long and painful train ride when no one had expected to him to.

Almost begrudgingly, they rolled him off to the surgical wing shortly after his arrival. Seeing his eyes rolling in his head as he mouthed a woman's name, a nurse squeezed his hand while taking his pulse. She promised him things would be better in no time.

The first round of surgery took seven hours. Bleeding was stabilized, ribs were set, and he was hooked up to a machine to aid in breathing. If he survived the night, he was due for a second round in the morning.

At the end of her shift, a tired and worn-out nurse patted Ray's hand as he came to. "It's over for now, and you survived. Rest while you can because there's more coming your way tomorrow."

⟪⟫

The muscles in her belly contracted into what felt like a wall of concrete for the twelfth time. Ignoring the pain as much as possible, Emma chewed on her thumbnail and stared in the direction of the phone. It had rung often enough throughout the day, but not for the reasons she wanted it to. There had been one call from a nurse a few hours prior, stating that Ray had made it through surgery, that he was connected to a ventilator to aid in his breathing, and that, for the most part, he was stabilized. His condition, however, remained critical.

Emma had pulled the phone from her father and begged to talk to her husband. Her pleas were to no avail. Ray was still unconscious. The nurse promised to call if there was any change.

Unable to take the waiting, she called the hospital three separate times between contractions; they had progressed to the point that she was now certain that she was in true labor. It was then nearing midnight, and Magdalene was begging her to go to bed to get some rest for the struggle that lay ahead.

Emma waved her off. "I have to try one more time, Mama. Once he comes to, I know they'll let me talk to him."

Once she finally got through, the nurse told her it was too late to attempt to put any calls through to patients.

Unable to hold it in any longer, Emma burst into tears. "You don't understand," she begged, trying hard to catch her breath between sobs. "I'm about to have a baby—my husband's baby. It's our first child. They say...they say he's pretty bad off. He's got to know I'm in labor. He's got to know our baby's coming into this world before he goes into surgery again in the morning. You've just got to let me talk to him. Please, I beg you."

Emma's plea worked. After a moment's hesitation, the nurse put her on hold and headed into the intensive care wing herself to see if he was conscious and able to take the call. After minutes of waiting and enduring the strongest contraction yet, Emma felt her heart soar at the nurse's words. Ray was awake enough to take her call. They were going to put the call through, and Emma was forewarned that it would have to be short. He was in no condition to wear himself out.

Emma held her breath and strained to discern the shuffling on the other line. Finally a weak, tired voice mumbled hello. Emma burst into sobs at the sound of it.

"Ray, dear God. Dear God. I love you so much. I know you're hurting, but you have to hang on. I'm having our baby, Ray. Right now or at least I will be. The contractions have been coming on strong for a while now. Can you hear me okay, Ray? I know I'm sobbing like a baby. I just can't stop it now. Are you there?"

Emma strained to curtail her sobs and hear into the silence of the line.

"You're my girl," Ray replied finally.

Emma burst into another round of sobs. Magdalene hugged her and asked if she should take the line. Emma waved her off.

"I'm having our baby, Ray. Our little baby's getting ready to come so we both have something difficult to do. I promise you that I'll bring our baby into this world safely. Now you just have to keep your promise to stay alive too, Ray. Do you hear?"

There was a shifting of sheets or words spoken too softly for her to ascertain. Emma's stomach lurched in fear, but she managed to curtail her sobs.

"If you can't speak, it's okay. You already promised me, remember? So I know you're coming home. I *know* it. We'll never be apart again once you do. You hang on for me, and I'll hang on for you. It's the only way to do this."

Emma pressed the phone to her ear so hard that it hurt. Finally she heard him mumble something that sounded like "Be safe."

"I will, Ray. Now get some rest, and tomorrow, things will be better. When I call you tomorrow, you'll have had your surgery, and I'll be introducing you to our baby. It's that simple, Ray. It's just that simple."

"It is that, isn't it?" came a faint whisper. "I love you, Emma."

Emma felt a wave of disbelief wash over her as the nurse came back online and told her that her husband had passed out from the effort of talking.

"He heard you," the stranger's voice insisted. "He heard you. Call again tomorrow when you and your baby are safe."

Emma hung up the phone and collapsed against the wall. The simple shifting of movement resulted in a gush of water hitting the floor. Emma stared at it in disbelief, at a loss to understand where it had come from. Her legs, feet, and nightgown were soaked. She looked to her mother who had covered her mouth with one hand.

Her father, who had been quietly listening at the table, lurched to his feet.

"Magdalene, get her to bed. I'll call Dr. Whitaker and let him know that her water broke and that the contractions are starting to come on strong."

Before she could move, a contraction ripped through Emma that was so strong she doubled over and vomited onto the water that was surrounding her. When she finished and the pain subsided, she wiped her mouth and stood upright again.

She set her shoulders and dismissed the look of fear in her mother's eyes with a wave of her hand. "It's okay, Mama.

It'll be okay now. We both know what we have to do. Ray has to stay alive, and I have to deliver his baby safely. Daddy says we're both strong as nails. We can do it. Together we can do it."

19

Birth and Survival

At 6:27 a.m. on May 26, 1944, Ray Dennis Rowe entered the world. For Emma, the night had been long, painful, and exhausting. But she had had a reason to endure the pain. She and her husband were united in struggles of birth and survival. Even from far away, Emma felt certain they were working together to accomplish these tasks that felt nearly impossible.

When her strength had all but given out, Dr. Whitaker encouraged her to push a few more times, and finally, progress was made. Shortly after, Dennis was born. He was beautiful. Her heart swelled with pleasure at the sight of him and at the feel of his soft skin against hers. Even knowing little about babies, Emma knew he was big before Dr. Whitaker cleaned and weighed him. Eleven pounds. Magdalene gasped and slapped her knee at the announcement. In all her years, she had never known a baby to be so big. And he was healthy too. He was pink-skinned and bright-eyed, and he had a healthy set of lungs.

Yes, Emma had certainly done her part, Magdalene insisted. "Now you rest, dear, and before long we'll have news of Ray, I'm certain."

She was right. Within an hour of Dennis's birth, his father, 150 miles away, entered a second critical surgery, focusing on his lower ribs, pelvis, and right leg. At noon the Givens' phone rang. Ray had made it through surgery, he was conscious, and he was on the road to recovery.

With tears of happiness, Emma finally felt she could allow herself to drift off to sleep. Beside her, in the bedroom she had known since she was a child, her baby slept wrapped tight in a blanket. She drifted off and felt as if Ray were beside her, holding her hand rather than so many long miles away.

Under the yellow florescent lights of the Kennedy Veteran's Hospital recovery room, Ray woke up to the sound of a soft, persistent beeping. Too weak to move his body, he shifted his eyes to take in the cumbersome machine beside him. He fought off a wave of panic as his lungs rose and fell in a false manner that he knew immediately was not his. The machine was doing his breathing for him, but the very idea of it was suffocating.

He remembered a kind nurse with yellow hair and soft hands leaning over him and reassuring him that things were going to be okay. She held his hand and spoke to him of a son—*his* son. Emma had done it. She had made it through the delivery and given birth to a baby boy. It was reason enough for him to hang on when doing so felt like an overwhelming task.

He remembered nothing of the accident, but he had been told enough details by the hospital staff that he could not get the self-conjured image out of his head. They had been on a night training session, and Ray had fallen into the path of a crawler truck. Two different doctors told him that there was no way he should have survived the crushing impact, but he did, so he very well should keep on doing so. Miracles of survival didn't happen every day, he was assured.

The first thing Ray clearly remembered after the accident was waking up and feeling like he wanted to die. His body was broken all to hell, and the pain was unspeakable. He was in the medical bunk in Mississippi surrounded by strangers, and dear God, they were drilling into his shattered leg. At that moment, he had wanted to die to escape the pain. He had wanted it desperately. When his body didn't listen, he vomited—nearly choking on it before the people hovering over him realized he had done so and helped to clear his throat. He had no memory of anything for a long time afterward; he must have blacked out.

He had come to again on a train. The male nurse seated nearby was leaving him alone, but the pain was still too intense to tolerate. His body jiggled in its cot as the train lurched along its tracks underneath him. It was too much pain to get a handle on. It felt like he was drowning in a sea of acid, only the acid wasn't attacking his skin. It was eating him alive from the inside.

Again, in the insanity of pain, Ray wished for death. At least a part of him did. Another part remembered his wife and a promise he had made, and he knew that he needed to endure the pain awhile longer. Ray had made a promise, and as long as it was in his power to keep it, that was what he intended to do.

For the most part, he only felt the memory of the pain now that he was in the hospital. He was groggy, numb, and nauseous. He felt like he was floating in a sea of water. Occasionally, a wave of panic would wash over him, and he would fear drowning in a room filled with breathable air. The ventilator's rhythm would become off-kilter to Ray's desires to breathe, and the panic would wash over him. When it did, he conjured an image of Emma, smiling down at a swaddled baby. It was his peace, and it held him until the wave of panic subsided.

That was how he began to tick off the hours and eventually the days. In the morning, the sun came in strong in the room's only window on the east side. By dinner, the shaded east side of the building grew so dim that the room glowed yellow in the artificial lighting. Ray drifted in and out of sleep and passed the first several days trying to detach from thought as much as possible.

By the tenth day, the ventilator was removed, and Ray's lungs worked on his own again. The pleasure of them doing so was enormous, and Ray felt empowered by it. It would be weeks or months until he could so much as roll over on his own, broken and bandaged up as he was, but his lungs were once again his to command. It was a beautiful thing for certain.

Without the ventilator, talking was easier, and Ray felt more aware of the world around him. The highlight of his day was when Emma called. She was waiting on pins and needles for Dr. Whitaker to clear her for travel. As soon as he did, Ray knew she'd be on the first train with her family and with his son on their way to the hospital to see him. He worked every day to get stronger so that the sight of him wouldn't be so troublesome for her.

The war was the talk of most of the soldiers in the hospital with him. Almost everyone there had been to the front and had stories to tell. Ray knew that no matter what happened, a part of him would never forgive himself for not being able to fight for his country or for his family when he had been so determined to do it.

Even if the war was still going on when he recovered, it would never be his war to fight. The doctors told him as much every time he asked. If he walked at all, he would walk with a severe limp. Such a limp would never be suitable for a soldier.

On the morning of June 6, Ray woke up to a hospital room that was literally buzzing with commotion. Who had heard word first, Ray never knew, but the other nine guys in the room with him all knew about the Normandy invasion before he did.

It was the biggest, most ambitious invasion by Allied forces yet, they told him. Ray felt his heart sink at the news. That big ambitious invasion in France is where he was supposed to be. That's where his buddies were. He was certain of it.

He stayed awake all day, even when exhaustion and the deep, piercing pain that never went away threatened to overwhelm him. He and his hospital buddies craned their ears to the radio and drilled every hospital worker who entered their room.

Ray thought of Martin and Jimmy and all the other guys he had grown to hold as dear in his heart as family during his twelve weeks of training. The biggest invasion of the war and they were there. They were there with thousands of other soldiers invading the beaches of Normandy, hoping to regain a stronghold in occupied France. They were his buddies, and even though most of the time he was skeptical as to the existence of God—or at least whether or not a God existed that listened to and answered prayers—Ray prayed over and over for the safety of his friends. Broken and strapped to a bed, there was nothing else he could do.

It took eleven days, but eventually Ray received the confirmation he feared for each of his friends, one by one. So many of the names he had first felt he would never learn at the onset of training—names he had eventually put with faces that had grown dear to him—he would never see again.

Eleven men of the fourteen in his bunk had died on the beaches of Normandy. As the days passed and the names of his friends were added to the list of the fallen, Ray felt sick and horrified. With each confirmation, he felt a part of himself die off. He was meant to have fought alongside his buddies. If he hadn't been run over, he'd surely have faced death with them on the beaches of Normandy.

He looked down at his broken body and shook his head. *What a miserable way to cheat death.*

20

A Real Family

Emma's suitcase was packed and ready two days before Dr. Whitaker released her and baby Dennis from his care. Dick Givens shook his head at the look of determination on her face after the doctor left.

"Am I to take it that we'll be leaving tomorrow then?" he asked. "It seems awfully early to be putting the baby through such a journey, but I know there's no holding you back now."

Emma shifted the baby in her arms and headed into the kitchen. "It's been nearly four weeks, Daddy. I'll go crazy if I have to wait another week to see Ray."

"I know, darling, but he ain't going anywhere for a while. He's alive and getting stronger every day."

"That may be true," Emma said, joining Magdalene in the kitchen and calling to him over her shoulder, "but you know as well as I do that the road before him is a long one.

It'll be months before they let him out of bed, and then he'll have to relearn to walk and care for himself. Besides, the journey is only 150 miles. Little Dennis will just have to get used to taking it every few weekends. At least he'll have the three of us to care for him."

"Mary will be wanting to go, if not this time, then next. This has been hard on her, and she has it hard enough already."

"I know," Emma agreed. "And without Ray working or sending home a soldier's pay, things will be harder on them for certain. At least Katherine, Lucille, and Earl are old enough now to do their fair share to help bring money in for their family. A few more years, and most of them will be out on their own. Then Mary won't have to work so hard to make ends meet."

Dick walked into the kitchen and draped an arm around his daughter. "It's all going to work out. You two have more on your shoulders now than a young couple ever needs to, but it's going to be all right. Ray's like a son to me too. Your ma and I have enough saved to help Mary out if she needs it. Right now, we just need to focus on helping Ray heal and come home as quickly as he can."

They sat at the table for a while, mulling over what to bring Ray. Certainly he'd be happy for some of the comforts of home. Now that he wasn't headed off to war, he might want a few personal items at his side.

When Dennis started to cry, Magdalene had a bottle ready. His sleep that night was fitful and kept Emma from getting much rest, but regardless, she was the first one up at the break of dawn.

"Ray ain't going anywhere, Emma," Dick protested at the sight of her dressed and ready to go as he headed for the coffee pot.

"No, but we are, and the sooner, the better."

The train ride from East Prairie to Memphis took the better part of the day with all the stops made along the way. By the time they had arrived in the city that was so much bigger than East Prairie that it took Emma's breath away, it was almost supper time.

Emma felt her chest constrict into a ball on the bus ride to the hospital. On the way up the elevator, it grew so tight that Emma wondered if she'd soon cease to breathe at all.

She was going to see Ray. She had a picture of him, injured and confined to a bed, in her mind's eye. It has been four months since she had last seen him. No doubt that whatever strength he had gained in training, he had lost in the long weeks since the accident.

With Dennis swaddled and clutched in her arms, Emma braced herself as she and her parents were led to his room. His eyes were closed when they entered as if he were dozing. Emma's eyes filled with tears at the sight of him. More of his body was covered in casts and connected to pulleys than wasn't.

Choking back a sob, she swept across the room. His eyes opened in surprise as she knelt over him, her large tears falling down onto his chest and neck. He swept her tightly into his arms. His own eyes filled with tears as well.

"Emma." Ray pressed his face into her hair, "I knew everything would be okay the moment I saw you. Shucks, I feel as if I could pull out of these casts right now and walk out of here."

Emma laughed and swiped at her eyes. "Ray, meet our baby. He hollered something terrible the last hour, but he's sound asleep now." Emma shifted her swaddled son, tilting his lower body so that his face was visible. He looks just like you, doesn't he?"

A dry laugh escaped, and Ray shook away the tears spilling down his cheeks. "He's too beautiful to look like me, Emma. He's all you, an angel just like his mama." His gaze fell on Dick and Magdalene, who stood quietly behind their daughter. He reached out a hand toward Magdalene. "It ain't worth getting worked up over, Magdalene. I'll be a bit of a gimp most likely, but I've long since been out of danger. Now it's just getting everything to mend and work like it used to. "I expect I won't be sprinting anymore, but heck, I was never much of a sprinter anyways."

Magdalene turned into Dick and sobbed into his chest a moment, and then she pulled herself together and crossed over to her son-in-law. "I couldn't love you more if you were my own, Ray. We're going to get you home as soon as we can."

Ray glanced at Emma and swallowed hard. "Do you believe in fate, Emma?"

Emma's black curls slid over her shoulders as she brushed away more tears. "I believe in you, Ray Rowe. And I believe in God. And he's been good to us saving you from something that everyone said you should have never survived."

"Well, I'm not so sure he believes in me, but I expect he believes in you. All them boys in my unit, well, only two of them are still alive. The rest of them have died on the beaches of Normandy, Emma. If things had played out differently, I'd be a goner too."

Emma silenced him with one finger, closing it over his lips and shaking her head adamantly. "I'm sorry for them boys, Ray, but you're staying with me. You have to. With you at my side, I can get through anything. We're going to be okay. *You're* going to be okay. There's three of us now. That makes us a real family."

Ray smiled and pressed his lips against her finger, and then he closed his hand over hers.

"We are, aren't we? We're a real family at that, Emma Rowe. It might not be what we expected, but we're gonna be together again, and that's all that matters."

21

The Fall

Life once again fell into a routine. Emma remained in her parents' home. The first weeks and months after her first visit to the Kennedy Veterans' Hospital, Emma was hopeful that Ray would soon join them. However, it was time that revealed the extent of his injuries the most to her. He was in and out of multiple surgeries and in a body cast for months. When the casts were removed, Ray was as weak as a kitten. He needed to relearn simple movements, to stand, and to walk. Every movement caused him pain. After weeks of pitifully slow progress, Emma finally felt confident that her husband would in fact learn to walk again.

What worried her the most was the subdued way he had begun to view the world—as if the crawler had squished some of his spirit along with his lungs and bones. When his eyes fell on his growing son during her short visits, Emma would glimpse the familiar tender light in them once more and feel confident that he would once again be the man she fell in love with. The burden of living when his unit did not weighed on him as great as his injuries. From his brother to his father and now to his comrades, Ray Rowe had been dealt more than enough loss than any one person ever needed to bear.

Summer passed, and Dennis grew big enough to smile, laugh, and grab a fistful of her hair into his plump fists. Emma prepared to return to her teaching position in the farmlands on the outskirts of East Prairie. It would certainly be a burden on them, but a necessary one now that Ray wasn't bringing any money into their household. Magdalene would care for Dennis during the day. Dick would drive her to work on his way to the McCracken Cotton Gin and pick her up on his way home.

She missed the home she and Ray rented on the outskirts of town, but she'd keep living with her parents until Ray came home so that she wouldn't be alone with the baby. She went by their rental house every few days to tidy up, water the plants, and get the mail. Usually Dennis and Magdalene accompanied her.

A week before the start of school, Emma opened the mailbox and saw the letter from the State Department of Education. She didn't think much about it at the time and had no premonition about opening it in her kitchen before they were to leave for her parents' house, but after opening it, she stared at the words in disbelief. Nothing sank in for a long moment.

Magdalene shifted Dennis on her hip and brushed her thumb over Emma's arm. "What is it, baby? You're white as a ghost."

Emma sank back against the counter in her kitchen. "I don't know who sent it, Mama, but it's a joke. It has to be a joke."

"What do you mean?"

"Only it's signed by someone in the Department of Education." Emma dropped the letter, her wrist too weak to keep it propped open before her. "It says regrettably I can't teach anymore. It says without a teaching certificate, I'm not qualified to teach my kids. It's not possible."

"Not qualified to teach!" Magdalene protested. "Why, who do they think they are? You made more progress with some of those kids last year than anyone ever had. A dozen parents told you so directly, Emma. It's a mistake. It has to be."

Emma crossed her arms over her stomach. "Ray's too tore up to work, and now they're telling me I'm not qualified to hold a teaching job. All my life I've swore I wouldn't end up in the poor house, but it certainly looks like that's where we're headed, doesn't it? How could we possibly not if they take away my job on top of what's happened to Ray? How can we possibly be dealt this right now? It isn't fair, Mama." Emma felt tears well up in her eyes. Frustrated, she stamped her foot and cleared her throat. "Well, I won't give up that easy. There has to be someone I can talk to about this. They'll be someone I can talk to who will make an exception. I know it."

Emma spent the next four days on the phone, talking to every Missouri official she could get a hold of. Unfortunately, the answers were the same everywhere. Times were changing. If Emma wanted to teach, she was first going to have to earn a teaching certificate. And that meant going to college.

The idea of doing so felt distant at first and unobtainable. No one in her family had ever considered going to college. Ever. But Emma possessed qualities that were college-worthy. She knew it to be true even though the idea of attending college terrified her. She was determined and diligent. School had always been easy for her. She was certain she was smart enough to learn whatever it was they felt a teaching degree would teach her.

"Well," Emma said finally, having slept on the idea a few nights. "It's settled, I reckon."

"What is settled?" Magdalene asked as she topped off her cup of coffee.

"Me and teaching. I'm going back to school to get my degree. With a degree, I could even work at the school here in East Prairie, I'll bet. You know it's been my dream forever."

"But college, Emma," Magdalene protested. "Of course, your father and I will support you and help with the baby as much as you need, but are you certain it's something you want to do? The very idea is so…I don't know…intimidating. But if anyone of my babies can do it, I know it will be you. Just make certain you can take the pressure, especially with caring for Ray once he comes home."

"I won't end up in the poor house, Mama, and I'm meant to be a teacher. I was a teacher for a year, and I was an awful good one. I know it. Those kids connected with me. Little Sally, Jimmy, and Fred didn't even know their letters when the year started. When it was through, they were comfortably reading McGuffey Readers. That was no small accomplishment."

Magdalene agreed. "You did at that, dear, for certain. Well, I can see you're set on this too. When do you intend to start?"

Emma shrugged. "Now, I reckon, if you're willing to help with Dennis. I might as well get through with the classes as I can while Ray's still gone and I'm living with you."

"That makes sense."

It was settled for Emma. She had taken a hit but was willing to stand back up and shake it off. In just a matter of days, she was signed up to take classes at the state university, which was a few hours' drive away. She was used to driving by herself and had no worry about making the commute twice a week in the Plymouth. It was a small sacrifice to have the life she was intended to have. Not everything was turning out to be easy, but it was worth it all the same.

⸺⬦⬦⸺

Emma's first year back to school flew by. Before she knew it, she was studying for her finals. Ray was still in Memphis, and his therapy was finally winding down. His doctors said he'd be coming home soon. He'd been a patient in the Kennedy hospital for nearly a full year, and they were more than ready for their long absence from one another to be over.

She did her best to visit him twice a month with her family and, occasionally, his in tow. When she arrived now, Ray was able to get out of bed long enough to take walks with her down the hall. They'd stay away from the room and view of the other guys as long as Ray could tolerate the pain that standing sent running through his hip and down his right leg. They'd find a quiet corner, and he'd wrap her in his arms. Emma would breathe in his scent and pretend that things were just as they used to be. Back when she spent her days teaching, he at the IGA, and they had long, happy nights together.

Afterward, she scolded herself for such selfish thoughts. Ray was alive. They had a baby. What more could she ask for? Dennis was thriving, and Dick and Magdalene were enjoying their time with their only grandchild. She and Ray would still have a good life together. They were just going to have to work harder for it than she had expected. Together they could do it. Together they could do anything.

As Emma drove to the university to take her year-end college finals, her stomach was in a knot. Her mother and Dennis were with her. Dennis, days away from being one, pumped his arms and cooed as the trees flew by. He loved sitting in Magdalene's lap and riding along in the car. Unlike many babies, Dennis didn't get carsick, so it wasn't imposing on him when Magdalene declared she wanted to accompany Emma to her finals.

Emma was able to take many of the courses she needed at home and then take her tests at the college. Earning her degree would take several years at this pace, but she could manage.

"Shucks, my palms are sweating, Mama."

Magdalene reached over and squeezed her knee. "Emma, you're smart as a jaybird. You're going to do fine on this test. I know it."

"Won't Ray be proud when he comes home in a few weeks, and I've already passed my first few courses? It'll be a good thing for him to come home to, won't it, Mama?"

"For sure it will."

Forcing down a wave of butterflies, Emma parked the Plymouth and leaned over to tickle Dennis's belly until he fell into hysterics.

"With a smile like that to return to, I can get through any test they throw at me."

"That you can," Magdalene agreed.

"Well, wish me luck. If you get tired of waiting around outside, just head into that building there, and I'll meet you down on the first floor when I'm finished."

"I will at that. Good luck, my dear," Magdalene said, planting a kiss on her daughter's cheek.

Magdalene watched Emma walk away into the big stone-and-brick building that was stately and collegiate and immensely intimidating to her. Her heart filled with pride as she watched Emma walk into her exams with her shoulders straight and her head held high. How she and Dick had given birth to such a bright and confident child still amazed her. Emma's smarts came from her father, Magdalene was certain.

Magdalene turned her grandson around to face her after Emma had disappeared inside the massive building. "Well, little Dennis, you're walking swell now while holding on to someone's hand. What do you say we take off through the lawn under the maples and ivy and have a nice walk through the campus while we wait?"

Dennis grinned at her voice and pumped his legs in excitement as if he understood her words. Magdalene laughed. She set him down carefully and took his hand as they headed across the parking lot toward the grass. Dennis stumbled while stepping up onto the curb, but Magdalene caught him up in her arms just in time.

"Watch it there, Dennis. We wouldn't want you to fall and hurt yourself, would we? Not when things are going so well. You're daddy's coming home, and we don't need you all bruised up. You'll be so happy you won't know what to do with yourself."

It was a ninety-minute exam. Even with Magdalene's stack of crackers and cookies that she kept in her purse, Dennis was tired and cranky once the allotted time had passed. As she stepped into the entrance of the large building that she had watched her daughter disappear into, Magdalene swept the baby up into her arms. "Just a few more minutes, baby-doll, then your mom will be driving again, and you can have a nap in my arms."

Dennis arched his back in protest of being held and rubbed eyes that were now rimmed with tiredness. From up above, Magdalene heard her daughter's voice echo off the marble walls and stairs down to her just ahead of several other students who must have been exiting the classroom with her.

"Thanks, but I came with my mother and baby today. Next time for certain."

Magdalene glanced toward the grand, rounded staircase and saw her daughter appear at the top of them. Just at that moment, Emma turned from her friends and looked down into the lobby. A smile lit up her face as she laid eyes on them. Shifting her belongings, Emma lifted her hand in a wave.

What happened next happened so fast that it didn't seem real to Magdalene. It was like a nightmare. She watched as her daughter stumbled at the very top of the massive stairs and tumbled downward. It wasn't real, Magdalene told herself. Those weren't her daughter's arms and legs flailing about as she hurtled down the hard marble stairs.

Steeling herself, Magdalene rushed forward with Dennis in her arms. She found tears spilling out her eyes when she needed to be strong.

"Dear God, Emma, are you all right?" Magdalene knelt over her, bile rushing into her throat.

Beneath her, Emma, who had been lying so still it seemed she might be unconscious, stirred to life and blinked her eyes. Magdalene placed her palm on her daughter's forehead and stifled a sob.

"How bad is it, Emma? Don't try to move. We'll send for help."

Emma shook her head and reached up to press her fingers against her son's plump cheek. "No, Mama. Just give me a second. I…I don't think anything's broken, just badly bruised. I just need a few minutes."

Emma's cheeks darkened in embarrassment as she glanced toward the crowd that had assembled around her. "I'm okay," she repeated.

"Should I get someone from administration?" a boy asked over Magdalene's shoulder.

"No," Emma repeated. "I'm fine, just embarrassed, and I need a moment to catch my breath." She laughed softly. "As a matter of fact, every inch of my body hurts just as badly as the next. If I'm not completely broken, I'll just be one big bruise for a few days."

There was a rumble of relieved laughter, and most of the crowd wished her well and continued on. One young man stayed and helped Emma to sit against the wall. After her back was supported against it, Emma waved him on. "I'll see you in September, Jim. Don't worry about me. What a laugh this will be by then."

Once he was gone, Magdalene exhaled deeply. "Emma, I haven't been so terrified since you were six and the last one up in that little tenement house just minutes before it washed away in the flood. I was so afraid your father would drop you. I thought I would pass out. I felt just the same way watching you fall down those steps. I'd gladly have taken the fall for you, if I could have, Emma."

Emma waved her hand dismissively and closed her eyes. "Don't be silly, Mama. It was just a little fall. I'm fine, really. Just give me a minute or two. I'm a bit dizzy, is all. How did little Dennis do?"

Magdalene shifted the protesting baby in her arms. "He's tired and wanting his mama back for certain, but he was wonderful. I expect he'll fall asleep as soon as the car is moving."

"I expect he will at that."

"Emma, are you certain you're okay? You're *so* pale."

"I'll be fine." Emma opened her eyes and shrugged it off. "Come on, Mama. Let's get home. I think I'm due for a nap this afternoon."

Magdalene chuckled. "Yes, you certainly are."

━━━◦◦◦◦◦━━━

Emma drove the whole way home but spoke very little. Twice she frightened Magdalene to the core when she admitted she didn't remember where they had been. Magdalene, who never drove, begged Emma to pull over. Emma dismissed her and insisted she was fine. She pulled over to the side of the road once and vomited. Afterward, she insisted that with the exception of an intense headache, she felt a good deal better.

As she settled back into the drive, she told her mother that she felt she had done well on her exams.

"Thank heavens, Emma," Magdalene said. "Twice earlier you didn't remember taking them at all. You about scared the daylights out of me."

"I'm okay, Mama. I just need to lie down once we get home."

Mercifully, Emma made it through the long drive to East Prairie. Magdalene plopped Dennis into his playpen, even though he started hollering immediately, and helped Emma to shed her shoes, skirt, and blouse. She darkened the windows in her daughter's bedroom, planted a kiss on her cheek, and shut the door.

She stepped out saying a prayer of thanks rather than one of desperation, having no idea of the condition in which her daughter would wake up.

Hours later, when they heard Emma cry out from her bedroom, Dick was home and Magdalene had been keeping supper warm for nearly an hour. They rushed in her room together, braced for the worst. Emma was never one to call out for help.

"Who made it so dark in here?" Emma asked. "I can't see a thing. What time is it?"

Magdalene switched on a lamp even though there was plenty of sunlight left in the room.

"Why, it's not even seven," Dick answered. "That must have been some fall. You've had your mama on edge all evening."

"Why aren't you turning on the light?" Emma asked an edge of panic in her voice. "Something doesn't feel right, and I don't like it one bit. Turn on the light so that I can see, please."

Dick's hand clutched his stomach in horror as he stared at the panic that was so evident on his daughter's face. "Magdalene," he whispered, "you stay here with the baby. I'm gonna get Emma to the hospital."

The following several days were a waking nightmare for Emma. Fear like she had never known gripped her insides and threatened to overwhelm her. It was unfathomable, existing while not being able to see. It was as if her eyes were sewn shut. She kept willing herself to see—demanding it of her body—but her body refused to listen.

Withholding the news from Ray as he prepared for his long-awaited journey home, Emma's parents took her from doctor to doctor. Depressingly, the news was the same. During her fall, Emma had hit her head hard enough to suffer damage to her optical nerves and retinas, and while some recovery of sight was possible, full recovery was far from probable.

As she adjusted to blindness, Emma discovered that her world was not totally black, but instead a field of gray with pinpoints of indiscernible light in the center. Time after time, she willed the small field of light to turn into an image, but it did not.

For the first time in her life, Emma felt a deep and terrible despair. It had been different for her when Ray was on his deathbed last year. Somehow, in her gut, Emma had known with great certainty that he would survive. He *had* to survive. She could see no other way. And now, now she couldn't see at all.

It was as if, along with her sight, her determination and strength had fled, leaving nothing but a hollow, terrified shell of a person. How could she live in a world where she couldn't turn over in the morning to admire the masculine definition in her husband's jawline as he slept on the pillow next to her? Or revel in the delight of her son's smile as he discovered so many new things? What would become of her, living in blindness? The people she loved would move on, and she would be there waiting to be guided from one life event that she couldn't experience to the next. What was her life to be if she couldn't witness it?

In the aftermath of her fall, Emma succumbed to despair. She turned away well-wishers, snapped at her parents when they attempted to comfort her, and kept to her bedroom most of the day. She cried out to her mother one morning when she came to check on her that, without sight, her life was worth nothing.

For the first time in years, Magdalene raised her voice to her daughter. Emma was sulking in the comfort of her bedsheets, but she started at her mother's tone. Magdalene crossed the room and sank down beside her. "Now you listen to me, Emma Jo Givens—I know you aren't a Givens in name any longer, so don't give me that look—you're a Givens at heart all the same. *What is life without sight?* You don't seriously believe that joy will be over for you, do you? You are the same smart and determined young woman you were before that fall, and no accident can take that away from you. You have the strength of heart that I've never seen in another person.

"Nobody knows *why* these things happen, but one thing is for sure, they almost never happen to people who can't handle them. You have the strength of a dozen people, Emma. You can bear this burden, and God knew that or it wouldn't have befallen you. What you can't see any longer, you can still hear, smell, taste, and feel. The world is still yours to experience, baby, you're just going to have to do it differently."

"But, Mama," Emma protested, "how can you sit there and tell me Ray will still love me the same? Dennis too?" She burst into the tears that she had been holding back for so long and sobbed out her greatest fear. "I'll…I'll be nothing more than a burden to them, someone they have to care for and wait on hand and foot. And Ray has more struggles ahead of him than he needs, with his frame so broken and falsely mended as it has been. What will this do to him, Mama? Dear God, what will it do to him?"

"Oh, fiddlesticks, Emma. That's the silliest thing I've ever heard. You know as well as I do that you'd have to be a great deal more than blind to allow anyone to wait on you hand and foot. You just weren't made to be waited on, Emma. Sight or no sight, you're still meant to move mountains."

Emma laughed bitterly and wiped her eyes. "How can I move mountains when I can't even find them any longer? How cruel a world is this? First, my job was taken from me and, when I determined not to let it sink me, now this. What am I supposed to do? What would you do, Mama?"

Magdalene laughed heartily and brushed her daughter's matted, silky hair away from her face. "Those are two very different questions, Emma. What I would do and what you would do will always bring forth different answers. The question you need to be asking yourself is, what are you going to do about it?"

22

Coming Home

The train rolled into the East Prairie station forty minutes behind schedule. Today Ray was coming home to East Prairie, coming home to Emma, to his family, and to his son.

After a great deal of trepidation, Emma had braced Ray for what had happened to her over the phone before his departure. She had wanted to tell him in person when she could be there in front of him and hope he would immediately see that not all of her was gone along with her vision. That there was still a great deal of Emma-ness to her and more of it returned every day. In the end, she had decided it was wrong to mar his long-awaited homecoming with the news.

Ray had taken the news well. He told her that he was sorry, that he loved her, and that it didn't matter to him.

"You've always been one to see with your heart anyways, Emma. And no fall can take that away from you."

Emma's father's hand was around her arm as the train pulled in. True to what her mother had told her, Emma heard the way the calls of the spring birds were muted by the scraping of metal against metal as the train came to a stop. She smelled the sting of diesel mixed with the perfume of budding trees and spring flowers. She felt the warmth of the sun on her shoulders and the cool breeze tickling her arms.

She felt the slightest tension in her father's fingertips as he announced that Ray had stepped off the train and was headed toward them. Moments later, she was being pulled into her husband's arms. Just as before, she fit against him perfectly, as if they were made to go together like the sun and the rain. The skin around her ear tickled as his warm, husky voice whispered in a way that only she could hear.

"Emma Rowe, dear God, I love you so much. You're mine, and I'm yours. In the end, that's all that really matters."

Emma felt the laughter bubble up in her chest as she wrapped her arms around him. She knew it then with undoubtable certainty. What he said—what her mother had said—both were true. Despite its hardships, life was truly beautiful. And she was determined to get busy living hers.

Epilogue

Considering that she was legally blind when she made the decision, it was one of the bravest decisions many around her had ever known. Emma Rowe was going back to college to earn a teaching degree, and she wasn't going to do it piecemeal either. She grabbed the task head-on and entered full-time. The decision would pull her away from her family—her husband, son, and parents—during the week, but Emma determined to enroll full-time.

The war ended just before her return to school, and once again, the world seemed to be a bustle of activity. Emma felt it in her bones—there was going to be a strong need for teachers soon, and teaching was exactly what she was put on this earth to do—with or without her vision.

Ray was hired back on at the IGA, and thanks to his dedicated service, he was promoted to the position of meatcutter. The skilled job paid more than other positions and, thankfully, also required a little less movement on his battered frame. As a result, he earned enough to put Emma through school and keep his family of three in their small rental home at the same time. It was a sacrifice, but one they were all willing to make.

Five days a week during the school year, Emma lived in dorms filled with students who were younger, single, and full of the promise of life. It was a struggle for her, blending in with them when she had a life so different, and on top of it, she could barely find her way around campus on her own.

The bright pinpoints of light she had first seen after the accident expanded somewhat, allowing Emma to see, albeit poorly, objects that were directly in front of her in faint detail. Using a magnifying glass and a flashlight, Emma could actually read a book, though it took her far longer than the other students. After a long night of studying, she looked forward to the walk down the long hallway to the vending machines for her reward—a Snickers candy bar and a bottle of Coke.

Time passed, and the Rowes fell into a routine. During the school year, Emma would spend her weekends baking and cooking up a storm to get her boys through the coming week without her. Then on Sunday nights, Ray drove Emma the long drive up to the college. To spare Dennis the trip, they usually left him behind with his grandparents.

Once at the campus, Ray would drop her off in front of the dorms, and sometimes—just to fit in with the other college kids—they'd linger in the parking lot and make out like they were still dating. Doing so made Emma nearly cry from laughter every time. Afterward, taking leave of him was the most wistful moment of her week.

It took two years, which were taxing on everyone involved, but Emma finally earned her teaching degree. She graduated magna cum laude in her class and was asked to speak at the graduation ceremony on account of her handicap and the obstacles she overcame to earn her degree.

Two days before her graduation, Emma received news that R. A. Doyle Elementary—the East Prairie school she was so intricately tied to—was hiring two new teachers the following year. Even before the interviews were scheduled, Emma was assured by the principal that she was a favorite for one of the positions.

The day of her graduation, Emma was greeted with fuzzy views of bright blue skies and a large crowd seated in the courtyard to honor the new graduates. Even though she couldn't make out their particular faces, Emma knew that many of the seats were filled with people who loved her—family and friends who had driven up to partake in the day and celebrate with her.

Emma crossed the stage cautiously and completely alone when her name was called. She reached out for her diploma from a robed man whose face she couldn't quite make out. She bit her lip as the cheers from the audience rose to a new crescendo.

She paused before heading offstage. She didn't know where her family was sitting, but she held her diploma up anyway. In a blur of barely discernible movement, she realized the audience was rising to their feet in unison.

Emma laughed and blew a kiss toward them. She knew her family wouldn't be able to hear her over the roar of the crowd, but she said what she suddenly needed to say anyway.

"This, Mama, is what I'm going to do about it."

Emma and Ray soon joined the First Christian Church in East Prairie. This set the course of their lives as disciples of Christ and leaders in their community. Emma found comfort and the determination to overcome the difficulties of her near blindness through her strong faith in God and enjoyed many years teaching the little ones in kindergarten. In a similar fashion, Ray's demons were calmed, and even his earlier skepticism in the existence of God was gradually overcome by serving in the church, becoming its youngest elder, where he served until his death at the age of eighty-six.